Edith Robinson

Penhallow Tales

Edith Robinson

Penhallow Tales

ISBN/EAN: 9783337023447

Printed in Europe, USA, Canada, Australia, Japan

Cover: Foto ©Andreas Hilbeck / pixelio.de

More available books at **www.hansebooks.com**

PENHALLOW TALES

PENHALLOW TALES

By

Edith Robinson

BOSTON
COPELAND AND DAY
MDCCCXCVI

CONTENTS

PENHALLOW

I.

" THE witches are after me! Mr. Winn,
Mr. Winn! The witches are after
me! They're tormenting me almost to
death!"

I put my hands over my ears to shut out
the hateful utterance, and involuntarily closed
my eyes also, as though I could thereby dispel
the mental picture that the words had evoked.
I was in the little attic chamber at the end of
the poorhouse, for which room I had begged
in order to be as far as possible from the inmates, and she was in her usual place on the
south steps, where the sun lay warm the
greater part of the day. Vital heat she could
not have had.

" The witches are after me! They're tormenting me almost to death!"

The words ended with a wail such as might
have been uttered by a lost soul condemned
to wander on earth through indefinite time.
In the darkness that I had created I only saw
more vividly a skeleton form — a mummy

rather, with a skin like brown leather, drawn so tightly over its hairless skull that the eyes, in which lingered most of the life of the creature who had once been a woman, seemed to be starting from their sockets. One could only guess at her height, for her form was bent nearly double, except when she would straighten herself in a moment of passion, and then hobble after some boys who had mockingly chanted, as they passed by, the rhymes that her name or her habits had suggested:

> "Old Sally Waters,
> Sitting in the sun!"

She was clad in the almshouse uniform, consisting of a short skirt of gray linsey-woolsey, and a round waist with a little cape reaching to the shoulders. A sharp watch had to be kept upon her to prevent her tearing off strips of this gown for the strange purpose for which she coveted them. No definite information in regard to the length of time old Sally Waters had been at the poorhouse could be obtained from the records, which, particularly in the earlier days, had been carelessly kept; the people in the neighborhood, who had owned their farms for generations, could only say that she had "allers been there," and that she looked as she did now when boys who had become grandfathers had called out to her as she sat in the glare of the July sunshine:

> " Old Sally Waters
> Sitting in the sun,
> Crying and weeping
> For a young man ! "

On stormy days, shutting herself into her bedroom, she would look over the contents of a battered little blue-painted chest that stood by the head of her bed, and which she guarded with jealous care: her treasure — probably charms against the witches that haunted her — was in the form of hundreds of knotted woollen rags that had been torn from her gown, and which contained cuttings of her nails. She had taken the most singular and unfortunate fancy to me, greeting me on my home-coming, a week before, with the words:

" You've been long gone, Martina ! "

And then, in some unfathomable emotion, she had begun crooning some gibberish to herself, varied by those wild shrieks.

Had she overheard my name in some chance mention by my father or mother? Dolt though old Sally Waters was, there were gleams of intelligence — cunning rather — that she now and then displayed, usually in connection with evading the watch kept upon her destructive propensity. It seemed to be a mark of favor that she had shown me her chest of disgusting relics, and even, with gestures commanding secrecy, displayed another charm that was likewise tied up in a gray flannel rag and worn suspended about her neck by a leather string.

Towards the other paupers she exhibited a frightful temper, varied at times by a ludicrous assumption of dignity and command. Her meals were brought to her in a corner of the dining-room apart from the rest, and in such terror were the other inmates of the house of the haunted atmosphere which old Sally Waters seemed to have created about herself, that none of them ever ventured to seat themselves in the straight-backed wooden chair that she called hers.

I hated the miserable creatures whose lives were spent in gossiping and quarrelling, whose sole ambition was to have the biggest pieces of pie on the days when mother had dessert for a treat. The very situation of the big, square, unpainted building, just below the crest of the hill, stifled me. On its other side, upon the gentle slope towards the river, was soon to be life such as I loved; but only cognizant were those in the almshouse of it all by the whistle and roar of the passing trains, many of which stopped at Penhallow station. This year the house from which the station was named — Penhallow Place — was to be reopened, after having stood vacant for forty years, transformed into a summer hotel by the aid of an army of carpenters and upholsterers.

Its many advantages were eloquently set forth in the circular :

" It stands upon high ground on the banks of the most beautiful part of the Merrimac, with fishing, boating, and bathing at the command of the guests. At the foot of the extensive lawn, in front of the house, shaded by magnificent elms of centuries' growth, is the highroad, leading, in either direction, to some of the most charming nooks and corners of New Hampshire. But what will, perhaps, as much as anything, recommend it to lovers of natural scenery, is its exceptional facilities for communication with Boston, it being but a little over an hour's ride thence, while the station is almost opposite the house."

Notwithstanding the beauty of the surrounding country, it seemed hitherto to have escaped the notice of the crowd of summer invaders. So the new hotel created a good deal of talk among the people about, and several girls whom I knew had taken places there as help. Mrs. Wason had offered me a situation, and I was glad of any opportunity to escape from the poorhouse. I was now taking the last stitches in the big white aprons that we were to wear, for Mrs. Wason wanted us to look tidy and nice before the Boston folks.

Two years before my home had been ten miles farther back in the country, in a little house surrounded by apple and pear trees that father had raised from the seed. In May it was like living in the midst of a bouquet. But the land was rocky and poor; father was getting too old to do the work alone, and it cost considerable to hire help; so when he had a chance to take charge of the poorhouse he and mother decided to make the change. I was away at school, and only sixteen. I spent the whole day crying over the sorry news. The idea of going home to the county almshouse was insupportable; so when vacation came I taught district school till the academy opened in the autumn. I intended to teach again the following summer, but a girl from Laconia got the place I wanted, so there seemed nothing for me to do but to come home and help mother with the housework and the sewing for the paupers.

It was even worse than I had anticipated, for I had not reckoned upon old Sally Waters as a factor in the almshouse life. But there were other reasons besides release from its hateful atmosphere that made me jump up and down with joy when father gave me Mrs. Wason's message; for to me Penhallow Place was enchanted ground.

II.

EIGHTY years before there had been no railroad holding on its string two or three bustling manufacturing towns; no highroad led past the lawn, and the thriving village of to-day was represented by a blacksmith's shop two miles distant. The almshouse did not then lurk upon the hill behind — an uncanny reverse side to the picture of light and love and laughter at Penhallow Place. There was a farmhouse or two in the country around, but for the most part the land for miles about belonged to the Penhallows.

The great white house loomed up, with its wings and broad verandas, the whole façade unbroken save by the portico, to which the driveway led, after sweeping around the lawn in front, which in those days was bordered by a double row of magnificent elms. That lovely unbroken stretch of greensward had been the pride of Madam Penhallow's heart. Now the lawn, despite the grandiloquent description of the circular, was not a quarter of its former extent, and the trees stood isolated on a dusty strip of land, known as "the Common," between the road and the railroad track. In the old days the driveway had wound a mile along the river's bank before it emerged from the private grounds, where now the village with its houses huddled thick together and an ill-smelling tannery had taken the place of field and meadow and woodland.

I had never wearied of listening to descriptions of the life in the great house eighty years before; how the rooms had been furnished, what great parties had been given, and how the children had looked and dressed, and what games they had played. They were always children to me, despite the fact that they had been grandfathers long before I was born. But best of all did I like to hear, and my grandmother to relate, how Madam Penhallow had looked; her picture was engraved upon my imagination from my very babyhood. It was her personality that exerted over me a charm that may have had in it something physical, for love of Madam Penhallow had been bone of her bone and flesh of her flesh to the girl — my great-grandmother — to whom she had been a kind though imperious mistress.

The story of that other life was running in my head now as I sat in my little room, while the voice from without now and again broke the thread of the retrospect:

"The witches are after me! They're tormenting me almost to de-a-th!"

III.

SARAH PENHALLOW was an only child; her father, Colonel Penhallow,— his name figures prominently in Revolutionary times, — worshipped her; so did everybody, for that matter, from her lovers to the hired help. She was the last of the name, and her father was anxious to see her married; he was a proud man, and it would have killed him to picture the big colonial mansion falling into a stranger's hands. His daughter had the family pride; some said the family temper, too. But, if the latter charge were true, it only served in those early days to make her the more high-spirited and lovable; for, if she were quick, she was also generous and forgiving, and that kind wins more hearts than do the cold-blooded, even-tempered folks.

As a child I was inclined to be fanciful and dreamy, and this tendency was increased by the solitary life I led. All my starved imagination centred about one personality — that of Sarah Penhallow. Not even the miserable end of a life that had begun in unclouded sunshine could shake my allegiance to her; about her was the whole atmosphere, so familiar to other children, wherein fairy godmothers, the "three wishes" of elfin munificence, flying horses, and glass mountains play their part. She was the beautiful princess for whom many a brave young prince would gladly have laid down his life. Whatever was good and true and lovely, whatever gave heart to the struggle to lift myself into a better and brighter world than the one in which the sordid struggle for existence held sole sway, was inspired by the ever-present image in my mind of that one woman.

There were gay goings on at the Place when on her twentieth birthday she was married. William MacNeil was poor, but as well born as herself; after his marriage he called himself MacNeil Penhallow. Soon there were two children, Ralph — there had been a Ralph Penhallow time out of mind in the family — and George. Then the old colonel died in a fit of apoplexy brought on by rage because his horse had not been properly groomed, and for a while it was quiet at the Place.

But before long the house was opened again, and the grand company came as before, in their own coaches, with outriders, from as far off as Portsmouth and Boston. The Penhallows were in the habit of going to the latter town for a few weeks in the winter and again for a few weeks when the General Court was sitting; but their hearts were always at Penhallow Place. The anniversary of their wedding day came in July, and the occasion was always celebrated by a grand ball. Come what might, they were always at Penhallow Place on that day.

They had two more children now — both boys. It was shortly after the birth of the last one that a change began to be observed in Madam Penhallow; some explained it by saying that she was growing like her father. She scolded the servants, and was often needlessly severe with the children; and then, to atone, would be indulgent beyond measure to both. She took offence at mere words with her friends, parted from several on trivial pretence, and seemed, by a certain aggressive bearing, to be constantly on the lookout for some ground of quarrel with all.

Her husband grew anxious about her health. Sometimes she would lie awake for several consecutive nights, and then would come a morning when her sleep would be so heavy that it was difficult to arouse her. She was restless, too, often spending the entire day in wandering from one room to another; again she would seem possessed by a very demon of work, and the embroidery needle would fly in her hands or the intricate lace grow beneath her rapid fingers; at other times she would sit for hours with her hands lying idle in her lap and a strange, fixed look in her eyes. There were those who shook their heads, but none liked to voice what was the thought of many. It was worse than either ill-temper or insanity.

Her husband repeatedly begged her to let him summon a doctor; she flew into a passion at the mere suggestion. It was not the first time that she had lost her temper with him, but never so violently as on that morning. The next moment she had her arm around his neck, and was upbraiding herself for her angry words.

"I will do anything you wish, love," she cried, "only I will not see a doctor."

"Then we will try a change," he urged. "Let us go to Washington. No wonder you have become depressed and nervous, living in this great house alone in the woods."

She put her hand over his mouth in her loving, imperious fashion.

"Do not say another word against Penhallow Place!" she cried. "I could not live long away from it. Blind and crippled and idiotic, I should still crawl back, through sheer instinct, to die in its beloved shadow. But since you wish it, Mac, we will go to Washington for a little while."

It was then early in the fall, and, despite her words, it was not until late in the spring that they returned. Through the following summer the house was filled with a succession of guests; there was ball after ball; there were picnics, riding and boating parties without number; and the feverish activity of the previous year seemed now to find its vent in social excitement.

Another child was born; he was named for his father, and grew up his living image, with a clear, pale complexion, blue eyes, and fair hair. He was his mother's darling, and in his presence her fits of passion were rare, for she could not bear to see the child shrink from her and raise his wondering eyes to her face. He did not cry, as other children might have done, but his grieved, shocked look speedily brought her to her senses, and a terrible fit of weeping would follow.

To a considerable degree he had his father's disposition, too, — gentle, yielding, singularly sweet and sensitive. He gave up his toys to his brothers without a word; but if one of them, in sport, tormented his pet kitten, the little fellow's eyes would flash, and his fist clench in Bonny's defence. No one with Penhallow blood in his veins could be a coward, but it sometimes seemed as though Mac were unfitted to fight his way through the world; however, it is often the gentlest nature that is capable of the stoutest resistance. The others were strong, sturdy boys, with whom it was take and fight, quarrel and make up, in hearty, boyish fashion; their differences left no rancor behind, for loyalty to one another was as prominent a characteristic of the Penhallows now as it had been long ago to Church and State, when to reward his " right faithful and loving subject, Ralph Penhallow," King Charles had granted to him certain lands in " ye New Plantation " that the family had held ever after.

Dating back to that visit to Washington, the children had become afraid of their mother; she was " so queer," the elder ones said among themselves. Only one person held the key of the mystery; and that person was her maid.

It was a sad time for poor Mr. Penhallow, although sadder days were yet to come. Mrs. Penhallow's temper was now common talk. Guests still came to the house, but the old-time feeling of open-handed hospitality was gone. It was like picnicking on top of a volcano.

Mr. Penhallow had always longed for a daughter; but little Mac was now ten years old, and it was unlikely that other children would be born to them. But when he heard, from his wife's own lips, that before long he would be a father again, he rejoiced as he had never done before in their married life, for from the first he made up his mind that the newcomer was to be a girl. He even decided upon her name. She should be called Elizabeth, after his mother.

Of late years the master of the house had shut himself up in his library. Naturally a quiet man, he had become a silent, even a moody, one. The children's laughter and frolic disturbed him, so they kept away from him, as well as from their mother. He had his own apartments, Madam Penhallow had hers; they met only at luncheon and dinner. Madam Penhallow's breakfast was taken to her own room. Her maid had orders never to disturb her morning nap, and all others were strictly forbidden to enter the apartment at any time. ·

Once Mr. Penhallow spoke to his wife of their new hope; perhaps he would fain have awakened some of the old feeling that had been between them. She checked him with a jeer at the unwonted display of affection, and, silenced, he returned to his library and his books; she to her own chamber — and her maid.

Much of the time there was spent in wild, long fits of weeping, that became more and more frequent as the time for her confinement drew near. If, in courteous, but never again loving, inquiry for her health her husband came to the door, he was met by the maid and the words:

"Madam Penhallow is lying down and must not be disturbed."

The child was born, a miserable, puny little creature, and when the mother looked at it she cried:

"Take it away! It is the visible sign and token of my sin!"

Those around thought that she spoke in the ravings of delirium. But her maid understood.

The father took the child — his Elizabeth — to his heart of hearts. Her nature was in as utter a contrast to her brothers' as was her physical being. They were endowed with keen, bold intellects that united the strong practical grasp of the Penhallows with the refined, scholarly tastes of the MacNeils. Little Elizabeth was hardly more robust in mind than in body. It took her days and weeks to master that which her brothers had acquired in one lesson. There was a hesitancy in her speech, and even the little that she said seemed to be an effort for her to conceive or to force herself to utter. It was to everybody's surprise and in refutation of the nurse's prediction that she had survived babyhood. Into her mother's presence the child was forbidden to come.

Yet with every year she grew more like her mother. But it was Madam Penhallow with the life gone; they were to each other like a crimson rose, fresh plucked on a June morning, and the same flower behind the glass of an embalmed funeral wreath.

She grew up at her father's side in the library. They took their meals there alone together; unlike the boys, she never disturbed him with an overflow of youthful spirits. She sat opposite to him in the big carved chair, speaking only in reply to some question; her big, dark eyes, that seemed to have absorbed all the life of the tiny little creature, fixed upon his face. Sometimes they would be seen crossing the lawn together. Elizabeth's solemn little steps keeping pace with those of her companion, her hand clasped in his. She never broke away, lured by the childish ambition of catching the big yellow butterfly that had just fluttered across their path, or

2

loosened her hold that she might fill her
hands to overflowing with the daisies and
buttercups that starred their way. It was an
unhealthy life for any child; for one with
Elizabeth's inheritance of morbid tendencies
it proved a fatal one.

There was an unlooked-for result that
sprang from the father's exclusive devotion
to his daughter. Madam Penhallow grew
madly jealous; her love had become per-
verted to the venomous passion that claims
all and would crush the very butterfly that
distracts a glance of the beloved one. The
servants whispered among themselves that it
would not be safe to leave Miss Elizabeth to
the mercies of her mother. If, by a seldom
chance, the two met, Madam Penhallow cast
such a look upon the quivering child as
made Elizabeth seek the library and sob out
her terror on her father's breast.

Three different lives were thus led beneath
the roof of Penhallow Place — in the library,
in Madam Penhallow's rooms, and in the
south wing, devoted to the boys, in which
was the only sunshine that had once flooded
the whole great mansion. Madam Penhallow
rarely left her own darkened apartments now,
except when she set out in her coach to return a few visits, or when, at stated intervals,
she threw open the doors for a grand ball;

for the custom was still kept up, mockery though it was, of celebrating the anniversary of their wedding-day.

There were only three boys at home now. Ralph had wished to go to college, and his mother had opposed the desire. One day he briefly bade good-by to them all, and left home on foot and alone, with no money in his pocket but that which he and his brothers had saved from their allowances. Arriving in Boston, his handsome face and pleasant ways aided him to find work without delay; his position was only that of errand boy, but he was well content therewith, for he did not mean to remain long a hewer of wood and drawer of water. Mr. Penhallow had attempted no remonstrance when his son told him his intention of breaking away from the home life. "Peace at any cost" had become the motto of the weary, disheartened man. Besides, he had Elizabeth; love for her had absorbed all his energy and intellect and paternal pride.

The following year George followed his brother's example, only he did not go through the empty formality of bidding his father good-by. Tom, shortly after, left the home-roof in like fashion; not, like his brothers, to seek his fortune in Boston, but to follow it at sea. Joe and Mac remained at home some time longer, spending the days in shooting, boating, riding, and, whenever they had money, in having "some fun" at Portsmouth. The two lads were growing up without restraint of any kind. There had been a succession of tutors at the house, but none ever remained long.

It was Ralph who came forward at last with the much-needed authority over the two younger lads. He had recently married; George was betrothed. Of Tom naught had been heard since he sailed in the "Bonaventure." There arose trouble out of the "fun" at Portsmouth. Accounts of a broken window, the pilfering of a shop, a scrimmage, and a double arrest found their way to the Boston newspapers. The two elder brothers went at once to Portsmouth, paid fines and costs and damages, scolded the culprits roundly, and insisted that both should come to Boston and henceforth consider themselves in their eldest brother's guardianship; to which mandate the two boys, somewhat alarmed at the results of their folly, at once yielded.

Joe was taken into the business, now known as "Penhallow Brothers," with the promise that good behavior should win for him a place in the firm. Partly by reason of the tight rein held over him, partly because he was ambitious, but most of all because his natural

character was honest and straightforward, he
devoted himself to his occupation, and soon
proved that his crop of wild oats was sown.

But " Little Mac," as his brothers still called
him, wanted to go to college ; and Ralph was
well pleased at the desire. So to school he
sent him, where the bright, eager boy soon
made up the years that had been lost at home.
By the time he was graduated from the law
school the firm of Penhallow Brothers, of
which Joe was now a member, had acquired
a world-wide fame.

IV.

THERE had been a terrible fit of rage when
Madam Penhallow received the letter from
Mac telling her that he, too, had left home.
She never afterward spoke of her sons, and
forbade their names to be mentioned in her
presence ; she displayed no emotion when the
tardy news reached New Hampshire that the
"Bonaventure" had been lost at sea, with all on
board. She had apparently become without
human instinct, save only her passion for her
husband, stifled though it was by another —
a master passion.

Elizabeth was nearly seventeen when the
first long act of the tragedy ended. She fell
in love with the only son of a once cherished

friend. The prospective match was in every way a desirable one. Hard though it would be to lose his darling, Mr. Penhallow longed to see her in a happy home of her own, for he shuddered at the thought of leaving her, in the event of his own death, to the mercies of the woman whom he called wife, but whom Elizabeth had never called mother. So he sanctioned not only the speedy engagement, but urged an early marriage. The girl was as happy in her new-found bliss as it was possible for one of her nature to be; and the reflection of her joy found its way to her father, creating yet another and closer bond between them.

Then it was that Madam Penhallow, who had hitherto paid no attention to her daughter's preference, suddenly awoke to what was going on, and, without even a pretext, forbade the engagement, and declared the doors of Penhallow Place to be shut against the young lover. There was a dreadful scene following this mandate, when Elizabeth fainted — she was wont to faint at the least excitement — and the young man uttered reproaches, hot and long, to Madam Penhallow.

"Wait a little while," said the father, ready to sacrifice even his daughter to his haunting dread of disturbance. "By and by she may yield."

Elizabeth, always ready to submit to his lightest word, did wait, but only for a little while. There were two meetings with her lover, at twilight, on the bank of the river; the second time was the last. The next day the woods were searched for her far and near, her lover leading the quest, but in vain. Then the father directed that the river should be dragged, and there, at last, Elizabeth's body was found, concealed beneath the shelving bank, in one of the places frequent on the Merrimac, near the very spot where she had bade her lover farewell.

They called it a misstep. Such a weak, frail creature as Elizabeth would not have had the courage to take her own life. Could the mother's will have usurped the place of the daughter's feeble powers, and relentlessly forced her to be her own destroyer? She had clung to her lover at their parting, sobbing pitifully:

"Don't leave me! She has always tried to make me do it. She will make me do it to-night!"

He had thought her hysterical.

The father uttered no reproach to his wife, but it was sad to see his tall, stooping figure, with its prematurely gray hair, drop a bunch of white roses into the open grave, and turning, with one heart-broken sob, give his arm, with his never-failing gentle courtesy, to the stately figure by his side.

But a week later there was upbraiding from him, for the first time in all their married life. No one dreamed that Madam Penhallow would give the usual ball that July, but the customary invitations were sent out immediately after Elizabeth's funeral. It was not till the very day before the festivity that the sound of preparations awakened the hermit in the library.

He sought his wife's apartments and implored her to give up the project. The ball was a sacrilege. It was cruel to him, in his loneliness and misery, with the only being on earth whom he loved torn from him, thus to make sport of death.

Jealousy of the living Elizabeth was as nothing compared to that which flamed up, at these words, against the dead girl. At last even Mr. Penhallow was aroused to the anger of the patient man.

" If you are determined to disgrace your name and your womanhood, I will not be here to witness the shame," he cried. " Elizabeth herself might well arise from her grave, in the dripping white garments in which she was driven to her death, and confront you with the reproaches that my darling would not utter in her lifetime. It is fitting

that you should rejoice over the consumma-
tion of your wishes." His hand was on the
latch as he spoke. " Good-by," he said.

She laughed scornfully.

" Good morning, if you like," she replied.
" You dare not leave me, as the others, one
by one, have done. You are not Penhallow
' by the grace of God,' but only by the grace
of man."

The taunt struck home. Perhaps at that
moment he realized how much there was
wherein he too had failed.

" I will be Penhallow no longer," he said.
" It was the mistake of my life that I ever
took the woman who bore the name. God
knows I have expiated the error."

" I will keep the first dance for you, as
usual," she called out mockingly after
him.

" I will be back to open the ball with you
upon your hundredth birthday, and not before," he made answer angrily, and raised
his right hand, as though in oath.

The preparations for the festivity went on.
Madam Penhallow took a last long look at
herself as she stood before the cheval-glass,
arrayed in her wedding-gown, that she always
wore upon these occasions, and, passing down
the broad staircase and through the hall, took
her station at the head of the ball-room. It

occupied the entire ground floor of the north
wing. She was mindful of all her duties as
hostess, but there was more than one guest
who noticed how often her eyes wandered
to the door as she talked of books, of poli-
tics, and of well-known people in Boston and
Washington.

But there were two subjects upon which
none were bold enough to touch. They were
the dead daughter and the absent husband;
and there was a chill upon all present, for it
was indeed as though they were "dancing
upon a grave." Midnight came, and Madam
Penhallow led the company to the supper-
room; in the early dawn of the next morning,
when the last guests were driving away, she
stood in the portico, the morning breeze not
daring to move a fold of her heavy gown or
to touch into the faintest ripple the fall of
its lace.

That was the last picture the world had of
Madam Penhallow of Penhallow Place.

She sold her horses; the carriages were
stored in the carriage-house; the furniture
was covered with linen, and the pictures and
mirrors swathed in netting. The servants
wondered among themselves as they did her
bidding. Some said that she was going
abroad; others, to Boston to live with her
sons; yet others averred that she intended to

leave her home to join her husband, who had sworn never to return there. At last, with her own hands she closed the blinds and drew the curtains all over the house, locked every door and window, paid the servants their wages, and dismissed them one and all.

Her sons, when the news reached them of their father's departure, made every effort to find him, but in vain. They thought he might have entered the army,— the war of 1812 was then going on,— but no information regarding MacNeil Penhallow was to be found. Only, strangely, none seemed to have thought of searching the records for William MacNeil.

Madam Penhallow remained alone at Penhallow Place. Not even her maid was allowed to stay with her, hard as the girl pleaded not to be sent away with the others. The door of the grand entrance was locked, never again to be opened during Madam Penhallow's solitary life in the mansion.

There she lived for ten long years, and no man, woman, or child ever looked upon her face again. The storekeeper — there had sprung up by this time a few scattered houses which they called a village — came once a week to get a basket holding a scrap of paper on which a few orders were written, that was placed by a side entrance, which he would replace with a basket containing the groceries

and eggs that had been ordered the previous
week.

Only one person ever entered the house,—
by the side entrance,—and that was her lawyer. She received him in the drawing-room,
where, by the light of a solitary candle, he did
the necessary writing, leaving any papers that
required signature. She meanwhile sat outside the faint circle of light, and her words
came as from an invisible presence. Man of
the world though he was, the lawyer shuddered at those strange interviews. Was his
client alive? He chid himself, on his home-
ward journey, for his uncanny fancies.

No longer with any one at hand upon whom
to vent her rage, it seemed to have turned
itself upon the whole outside world. In the
darkness the venom increased, as is the way
with all noisome things. Her contentions, her
lawsuits, were never ceasing.

As the village grew, strange stories were rife
about fierce Madam Penhallow. She was the
bugaboo of all the children for miles around.
" Ma'am Penholler 'll git yer ! " was the threat
of impatient mothers. Even grown men gave
the mansion a wide berth at nightfall. It was
rumored that at midnight her figure had been
seen among the graves in the family burying-
ground, adjoining which the poorhouse was
afterward built.

Seven miles away a community of mills had sprung up, and there were contests about water power, and a lawsuit because the Merrimac, as it flowed by her grounds, had become befouled with the factory refuse. But the town grew, and the factories increased in number and extent, and the mill-owners built houses on the outskirts of what was now a thriving city, and there followed other contests about rights of way, a railroad here, and a boundary there. Sometimes there were three or four lawsuits of "Penhallow *versus* ——" going on at once. They all ended in one way — a "verdict with costs against Penhallow." At last even the house and grounds were mortgaged to sustain her in her resolution that the highroad should not be cut through the lawn. But that contest, the longest and bitterest of all, likewise came to an end, and with it came the knowledge that there was not enough money left even to pay the interest on the mortgage on the mansion.

My great-grandmother had married immediately after leaving Madam Penhallow's service, and had since lived on the secluded little farm. It was not until weeks after the end was reached that she heard how the mortgage on the Place had been foreclosed, and that there had been an auction of carriages and

household effects, and even of Madam Penhallow's personal wardrobe. For the first
time for many years the grand entrance was
opened, light was let into the house, and
human footsteps and living voices sounded in
the rooms.

Madam Penhallow sat alone in her own
chamber while the auction was held in the
ball-room beneath; she could hear the auc-
tioneer's voice offering for sale her heirlooms,
with the jests which, it was supposed, made
the sales livelier. A wealthy mill-owner —
his father had been a stable-boy in Colonel
Penhallow's time — bought the mansion, and
the valuables were scattered far and wide.

Those closing scenes were forty years ago,
and since then Penhallow Place had never
been occupied save for two brief periods. The
first was by the mill-owner, who soon left
the house. People shook their heads at the
alleged reason — that it was damp. Later it
was used as a boarding-house for the laborers
when the railroad was built. No one knew
what became of Madam Penhallow. Her
sons, through their lawyer, who attended the
sale, offered her a handsome annuity. She
tore the letter to pieces and sent back the
fragments for answer. Whither she went,
when and how she died, none ever knew. It
was a strange story, whose inner meaning my

grandmother told me alone, as she lay upon her death-bed.

The evil had begun in Madam Penhallow's taking opium for sleepless nights, after her first children were born. The small amount with which she had begun soon losing its effect, the quantity was gradually but steadily increased. There were terrible struggles to free herself from its chains when she first began to realize what a hold the habit was getting upon her. But the craving was irresistible, and the yielding to its demands came after ever weakening efforts to assert her will. More than once she was on the point of confessing all to her husband and begging him to put her under restraint. Had his man's will been equal to her woman's strength of purpose, all might yet have gone well with her, fighting as she was for her husband, her children, and her home.

But already the weakness of his nature had been revealed to her, and she turned aside from the support of a broken reed. Besides, how could she acknowledge that she, with the will upon whose strength she had openly prided herself, was not strong enough to control an appetite !

The passion grew stronger and the struggle weaker. Days and nights were passed in stupor, the faithful maid on guard in the dressing-room. In those days the opium habit was almost unknown, and Madam Penhallow had unusual opportunities for obtaining the drug, while it was not suspected that she was a victim to the fatal craving.

So she lived and passed away, and all the world held her memory in opprobrium. All but one — her maid's great-granddaughter. At odds with her very nature, had she indeed any chance in the struggle, from the beginning to the bitter end?

To-morrow Penhallow Place would be filled with people again. The curtain had gone down on the tragedy, and the bell had rung for it to go up on the farce.

V.

"THIS is your table," said Mrs. Wason, as I followed her brisk steps down the long dining-room. She was a woman with "faculty" written all over her; in her beady, snapping black eyes, in her scanty hair brushed smoothly back from a shining forehead to be twisted into a hard little knob behind, and in her bony hands with their fingers worn to glassy smoothness away from the red knuckles. If any one could make keeping boarders pay, it was Mrs. Wason. "My best folks sit here," she added,

" an' I calkerlate as how you could do the waitin' smart as any on 'em; an' you look kind o' tasty an' spruced up in that apron."

She went on assigning their places to the other girls, while I stood by my table, waiting for the folks to come in to supper. The gong had sounded, and there were one or two guests standing by the door. The hired help had been busy since four o'clock that morning, making beds, filling pitchers, and getting things in order generally. Some of us had placed flowers in the various rooms, to try to have the house look cheerful and homelike; for in spite of the fresh paint and the new furniture there was a kind of chill in the air that made us look over our shoulders in the passages and hurry on the stairs. It would have been as much as our places were worth to mention this fear to Mrs. Wason, for she knew it did not take much to give a house a bad name, and we had all been charged not to breathe a word of the old stories to the Boston folks.

The rooms that were formerly Madam Penhallow's own were in my charge, and I had put roses in every available nook; on the dressing-table was a glass pitcher, crowded with our own " thousand-leaved " variety, which blossomed so luxuriantly in our garden on the hillside farm. Early the day before I had gone home with a boy who drove through the neighborhood to collect milk from the farmers. We used to play together at the district school, but he had grown bashful since those days, and I don't believe spoke a word, except in answer to a question, during all the drive over.

You could not find such roses as ours in all the country round. My great-grandmother had brought a slip of the bush with her when she left Penhallow Place. The garden back of the mansion had long ago run to decay, and not a vestige of what had been Madam Penhallow's favorite flower was to be found there now; but the tiny slip had thriven in our garden, and every year covered the back of our cottage with its June glories. It seemed as though it were for Madam Penhallow herself that I was bringing back the flowers. It was strange how the conception of her as of a living personality clung to me. But then mother had often chidden me for being fanciful.

A stream of people had entered the dining-room, the ladies arrayed in bright summer gowns, the gentlemen walking with alert steps and with heads erect. None of the men to whom I was accustomed carried themselves in such a way. Mrs. Wason was showing them to their places. The words that awoke me from my dream were uttered in her thin, high-pitched voice.

"Will you sit here? Martiny will wait on you. This is Martiny."

I took a step forward to draw back the chairs, and then stood petrified, staring at the new-comers, like the awkward country girl they must have thought me.

When and where and how had I seen that woman before — seen her with more than a mere passing glance; ay, and held converse with her, not once or twice, but many times?

She was tall — above the common height — and broad-shouldered, yet so well proportioned that she struck one as slender. She was pale, and there were dark rings beneath her beautiful gray eyes; her hair was brown, of curiously different shades. In the deepest tints it was dark brown — not reddish, but pure brown, paling here and there to a lighter shade, while in the thick coils that lay about her head were rings and gleams of gold. Where had I seen hair like that before? Hers and no other's it must have been, for, search as one might, how often, in a lifetime, could one find such softly shaded masses, lighted up with gold? Her mouth was the loveliest feature of her beautiful face. One lip had a fashion of curling as she talked. Her chin was square and firm, but soft and feminine too. She wore a gown of yellowish brown of some soft silken stuff. Her neck was bare in a tiny point in front, and in the folds of the lace was one of the thousand-leaved roses. Her whole appearance was familiar to me, even to the ring on the hand that lay lightly on her companion's arm. It was a ring set with a rough gray stone, encircled with diamonds.

The gentleman belonged in the picture too, although his face and figure were not so vivid as were the lady's. He was of about her height, with fair, wavy hair, a slight mustache, and blue eyes that never left his companion's face as she talked eagerly upon some apparently engrossing theme. Her voice was familiar too, as its tones came to me with their pure quality, and now and then, as she warmed with her subject, with inflections that were not shrillness, but were like chords of a yet purer quality. Possibly the familiarity of face and figure might have been explained by some coincidence, but the voice I had heard before, yet when, or where, or how, I did not know.

I put my hand to my forehead in the painful struggle to recall where I had heard tones that were surely hers — far-off, haunting tones, with their silvery cadences now and again glancing into shrillness. No, not shrillness.

Such a voice as that could never become, even in the course of years, sharp and ear-splitting, penetrating walls and cleaving the air, however one might seek to shut it out. Why was it that I felt myself all at once in my little attic chamber? I was growing dizzy.

I clutched the back of the nearest chair. The sudden motion broke the spell. I could see that the girl at the next table, who had overheard the complimentary words Mrs. Wason had spoken to me, was looking pleased at my awkwardness.

The lady before me drew back her chair herself, with the hand upon which was the curious ring.

" So this is Martina? " said she. " Thank you for the roses. I could not leave them all behind, you see. I hope that Mrs. Wason has as good a welcome for us here, for we are hungry."

I told them, haltingly, what we had for supper.

" Hot biscuit and tea for two," she ordered promptly.

" Sarah, you must not eat hot biscuit, and the doctor forbade tea, unconditionally," said the gentleman earnestly. " Let me order toast and milk for you."

" I detest milk. I am hungry, and will have what I want."

I hurried to the kitchen, where Mrs. Wason was everywhere at once, breaking up pans of biscuits, turning pancakes, and taking muffins and waffles from the stove. Instead of giving her my orders, I questioned, breathlessly:

"Mrs. Wason, who are the folks at my table?"

"Lor', child, how flustrated yer be," said she. "Them's Mr. and Mis' MacNeil Penholler."

VI.

I WAS helping Mrs. Wason iron some of the ladies' fine skirts, my grandmother having taught me how to clear starch. Some of the girls were afraid of doing more than they had hired out to do, for Mrs. Wason not only drove herself, but expected every one else to drive, even if they were not bound anywhere in particular. The original laundry was not large enough for the present needs of the house, and the old ball-room had been utilized for that purpose. Tubs had been placed along one side of the room and long ironing-tables upon the other, with a stove at each end on which to heat the flat-irons; the long windows, opening on the piazza, afforded easy access to the drying-ground back of the house. This was the first chance that I had

had to ask the question that had been hovering on my lips for the past three days.

" Be they related ter the folks as used ter live here? Yis, they're the great gran'children; he's Hon. MacNeil Penholler's gran'son, an' I've hearn tell is the livin' image of his gran'pa. Hain't she hahn'some? Yer kin see the real lady in her. Pity she hain't more rugged. 'Twould ha' been better for her ef she'd ha' be'n reared in the country, on good, healthy victuals, beans an' pork an' pie, 'stid o' the new-fangled dishes that Bostin folks like. She's got dyspepsy consid'rable bad. I was a-tellin' of her t'other mornin' how my son's wife's appetite got so nippin' after she'd buried Jemmy that she couldn't relish a dish o' beans an' was never even pie-hungry. All she lived on was milk; she was a powerful hand to drink milk— used ter say she b'lieved she never was weaned. She took 'Turlington's Balsam.' Three drops on a lump of sugar ev'ry mornin' until she could stumick a teaspoonful. Now she's as rugged a woman as yer'd want ter see, an' thinks nothin' of her big washes an' the cookin' fur seven children an' all the men-folks. She sets a store by 'Turlington's Balsam,' I kin tell yer.

" I hain't got no faith in doctors, but seein's b'lievin', an' so I tol' Mis' Penholler. But she's everlastin' set, an' I don' b'lieve minds

the doctor any more'n suits her high-mighti-
ness. She has nooraligy, too, all down her
back; but when I tol' her of how I knew a
woman who'd cured folks by holdin' of their
heads, an' all they had ter do themselves was
jist ter have faith, she laughed as though she'd
die. The doctor calls her ailment nervous pros-
terration, an' she says his prescripture-on is
milk. Beats all what some folks will b'lieve.

" They was only married las' fall, so she an'
her husband set consid'rable store by each
other yit; the doctor said she must git somewhere where it was high an' dry an' there was
pine breezes instid o' salt ones. An' she said
she wouldn't leave Bostin unless her husband
could be with her; between yer an' me, I
rather guess it's she who's master. But when
she saw the picter of the Place in the cir-
cler an' how the steam-cars come up to the
very door, as yer may say, she made up her
min' on the spot that she would go ' home,'
as she persis' in callin' Penholler Place. She's
cur'us enough 'bout the house, an' asked me a
sight o' questions 'bout the rooms. I b'lieve
she actyerally thought as how I could remember back t' her great-gran'ma'am's time.

" Yer'd oughter see her eyes open when I
tol' her that yer great-gran'ma'am was Ma'am
Penholler's own maid, an' that yer folks had
tol' me that yer was her livin' image.

" Be yer through? Ef I kin do yer a good
turn, Martiny, I'll not forgit. 'Tain't many
as kin starch lace an' muslin like yer an' me,
ef I do say it! "

VII.

EVERY morning Mrs. Penhallow would accompany her husband across the lawn to the
little railroad station and remain on the plat-
form till the train was out of sight. The train
by which he returned arrived at six o'clock,
and at half-past five Mrs. Penhallow, arrayed
in one of the lovely gowns of which she
had such a store, would be sitting at her
window watching for the first faint cloud of
smoke.

I liked to watch them from my post in the
dining-room, as with linked arms they slowly
crossed the lawn. Once or twice Mr. Penhallow was detained in town until ten o'clock,
but she was at the station, as usual, to greet
him, while she had delayed her own supper
that they might partake of it together. One
morning, at breakfast, I noticed how red her
eyes were, nor was it possible to avoid over-
hearing some of the words that passed between
them. She had a high way of disregarding
that which holds most people in check — the
thought of what folks may say.

" Don't go, darling."

" But I shall soon return, Sarah."

" Let somebody else go; I want you to stay with me."

" No other person can attend to this business as well as I. New York is not so long a journey from here that you will have time to miss me before I am home again."

" Stay with me. Just this once. Don't leave me, Mac, dearest."

But in spite of her persuasion I saw that he had his travelling-bag with him as they crossed the lawn; from her gestures it was evident that she was seeking to detain him to the very last. The morning following his departure she sent word for her breakfast to be brought to her room. I laid upon the tray some branches of swamp pinks that I had gathered near my old home that morning. Harry had driven me over several times of late. Mrs. Wason let me go whenever I asked, on condition that I was back in time to wait upon the breakfast table.

" Come," said Mrs. Penhallow's voice; and I entered.

She was in bed. Her arms, bare to the elbow, were flung over her head, and her hair lay in masses upon the pillow. I drew a table to the bedside, placed the tray upon it, and was about to withdraw. '

" Don't go," she said listlessly. " I want
to talk with you."

So I sat down in the chair she indicated,
and waited till she had sipped the strong
coffee that she had been so particular in
ordering.

" Thank you for the flowers," she said presently; " you keep my room like a garden.
Did those grow near here? " raising the pinks
to her face.

I told her shyly where it was that I had
gathered them, as well as the roses.

" Do you really take all that trouble to
bring me flowers? You are very kind,
Martina."

" I love to gather them for you," I said
impulsively.

" They came from your old home, you say?
Tell me about it."

I forgot that she was one of the fine Boston
folks, and that I was only a poor country girl,
and was soon describing my home, and even
telling her of my grief when I heard that father
had sold it and gone to the poorhouse. Em-
boldened by her interest, I went on to tell her
about some of the paupers, concluding with a
description of old Sally Waters, who sat on
the south steps all day, shrieking at intervals
about the witches who " tormented her 'most
to death."

"Poor old woman, who knows what Furies may be pursuing her from out the shadows of the past!" said Mrs. Penhallow, gently. "It was but a sorry home-coming for you, Martina."

She detained me some time longer that morning, listening and asking questions. She had not been feeling as well as usual, she said, and after lying awake till dawn had then fallen into a heavy sleep.

She suffered terribly at times from neuralgia; some nights she walked up and down the room until early morning, when the pain would lessen. But no matter what the agony had been, she always appeared with her husband at the breakfast table. She was not even looking as well as when she first came to Penhallow Place, despite the "healthy situation and pine breezes." After that morning when I first talked with her she took considerable notice of me in one way or another, and when I took her breakfast to her room, which I did whenever business had called Mr. Penhallow away overnight, she would bid me remain — at first, I think, from a desire for any diversion, but after a while I am sure it was because she was really interested.

I supposed, for some time, that her husband's absence was the reason for her non-appearance at the breakfast table; but by degrees I began to suspect that something was wrong about those morning naps, she was so drowsy and heavy-eyed, and would so eagerly drink the strong black coffee she always ordered. It was later than usual one day when I entered her room, and she was half asleep, but aroused herself to say, as I placed the tray on the table:

"Is that you, Martina? Give me the coffee."

It was partly, perhaps, because the story of Madam Penhallow was so familiar to me, and because Mrs. Penhallow was so inextricably tangled up in my mind with the story of long ago, that the dawning truth grew clear to me in a flash, and I cried:

"Oh, don't!"

The cup at her lips was replaced in the tray, and there was both astonishment and anger in Mrs. Penhallow's tones as she said:

"Don't drink coffee? You forget yourself, Martina."

"No, no; I mean — don't take opium."

There was a full half-minute's silence.

"What do you mean?" she said haughtily. "I have encouraged you too much by listening to your prattle. I take nothing of the kind." And she drained the cup at one draught.

But she had inadvertently denied more

than she intended. With a Penhallow truth was truth, without argument or sophistry.

"I take morphine," she said; "and what objection have you to my doing so, pray?"

"Please don't," I begged. "I am afraid that some day you might take too much."

Her lip curled scornfully.

"And you believe all those old woman's stories? Doubtless morphine might be dangerous in the hands of an ignorant country-woman, but I am not likely to blunder. Are you afraid that some morning you will bring your flowers and find only an unpleasant body to which to offer them?" Her scornful tone changed as in silence I took the tray and turned to leave the room. "What can I do?" she said impatiently. "You don't know the temptation. The pain is horrible. It torments me almost to death!" And the sharpness of her voice fairly rang through the room.

I had dropped the tray, and, unheeding the broken china, stood regarding her wildly. When had I heard her voice before, strained with agony, sharp with mingled despair and defiance, utter those very words?

The strain was too much for my self-control, and I burst into tears.

"There, Martina, don't take it to heart," said Mrs. Penhallow, in her usual careless, imperious tones. "You meant no harm.

That is all I require this morning; you can go now." And I went.

It was of Madam Penhallow that she liked best to hear, and I to relate, in those confidential hours in her room.

"You do not know the hold that she has always had upon my imagination," she said, one day. " It has become stronger than ever since I have lived in this house. None of us ever dared question our grandfather about the strange story that we vaguely knew was connected with Madam Penhallow.

"One day I was rummaging through some old chests in the store-room, when I came upon a miniature of her by Malbone. My likeness to the pictured face was apparent even to myself. I could fancy at times that the strong will and wild passion still linger in these rooms, ready to exert their influence over those whom, by birth and blood, she may claim. I cannot believe that she would have been content to give up her sway with life."

Mrs. Penhallow talked oddly sometimes. Often, after leaving her room, I would hurry through the corridors and run down the stairs, sure that a tall, stately figure, in the robes of eighty years ago, was gliding after me.

"Do you mean that you think her ghost is here?" I asked, one day.

" Heaven forbid ! " she laughed. " Have I been frightening you by my vagaries? I was only wondering how much influence mind can have over mind, even though one has been for a half-century what men call dead."

I did not know what she meant. I thought a ghost was a ghost, but she seemed to consider that there was something vulgar in that idea.

Some Sunday, she had said, she wanted me to show her and Mr. Penhallow about the mansion, for I knew its every nook and corner, and what purpose each room had served in the old time. The first Sunday slipped by, and on the second they went to church in the morning, and in the afternoon took a long walk. But the following week Mrs. Penhallow sent for me and reminded me of her wish.

" You know that these rooms were Madam Penhallow's own? " I began.

" There is a horrible depressing influence about them that would have told me, even if Mrs. Wason had not," she returned impatiently. " No, Mac, I cannot shake off the feeling that something is about to happen."

Her words were evidently in continuation of a conversation that my entrance had interrupted. She was walking excitedly up and down the room. Mr. Penhallow was seated, with a newspaper in his hand.

"Are you oppressed with a haunting sense of impending evil?" he questioned gravely. "That is it, exactly," she assented eagerly. "I never experienced the feeling before, but, strive as I may, I cannot drive it from me."

"Are your dreams troubled, your sleep restless? Are you haunted by strange fancies and morbid imaginings in your waking hours?"

"All that, Mac, and more. I am tormented almost to death! Don't look so wild, Martina! Let us leave this hateful place," she went on, too excited to see that her husband was laughing behind his screen.

"Then take 'Swinton's Specific!'" he concluded, pointing with an air of mock conviction to a newspaper advertisement he had been reading. At first she did not know whether to be angry or to laugh, but at last she chose the latter course.

"If you would leave tea and coffee alone, you would stop having presentiments. Dyspepsia is answerable for much of the bigotry and superstition of this world," said Mr. Penhallow.

"Who knows but what, in time, I may come to put faith in 'Turlington,' ghosts, and the faith cure!" she returned gayly, slipping her hand through his arm. "Come, let us go. If we encounter the traditional white-robed

4

figure, clanking chains and diffusing sulphuric fumes, we are three strong and can surely lay her. Martina is actually pale listening to our rambling talk."

I led the way through the state rooms. General Lafayette had slept here; Daniel Webster had once occupied this apartment for three days. Count Rumford always had this room, with its view down the river. These rooms had been known as " Bachelors' Corridor." The last apartments we visited were those in the south wing, where each boy had had a separate room, except Ralph and George, who always slept together. This corner room had been " Little Mac's." I stopped, blushing, for I had forgotten, in my earnestness, that I was not speaking of a golden-haired little boy, but of Hon. MacNeil Penhallow, who had made famous speeches in Congress and had been sent abroad as minister to more than one foreign court.

"Dear little fellow! " mused Mrs. Penhallow. " Can't you see him, Mac, in his velvet knee-breeches, his wide sash, and his yellow curls? I wonder if his mother kept a lock of that shining hair in her fierce old age? "

" I wish that we could indeed have met her in the corridors, overthrow though it would have been to our Boston scepticism, for with

all my heart I would have given her the forgiveness that her Little Mac would have
granted so freely. He could never hold rancor, you know."

" And I know one who is as like him in
spirit as in form and face," she returned,
softly.

At the door of their own room Mrs. Penhallow turned to me.

" I have been telling Mr. Penhallow about
your old home," she said. " We will go there
with you to-morrow morning."

" The wagon has no springs, and we shall
have to start at four o'clock," I faltered.

" That is the way and the time we want to
go. It would destroy all the savor to order
the horses and carriage and go at an orthodox
hour. Be sure and wake us in time."

So I ran downstairs to tell Harry to put an
extra seat in the wagon. He had been helping Mr. Wason lately with the chores.

VIII.

THE road led down the village street and
across the big iron bridge, till presently it
brought us to the open country. We drove
past belts and groves of pines and stretches of
woodland; then, for a while, along the high

river bank, with the water gleaming through its fringe of birches and alders. Emerging again into the open country, the road led past fields that stretched, on either hand, to far in the distance.

The tall pines that now bordered the road shut off my old home from view till we turned into the rocky driveway and the next moment were in sight of a long, low house. Apple and pear and cherry trees covered the slopes about. Farther up the hill lay the garden, in which vegetables and flowers grew together in friendly juxtaposition. Over there, by the stone wall, were the beehives, and there was the well, whose site father had discovered by means of a witch-hazel wand. The last place that we visited was the little pool by the hedge.

" I do not wonder that you love your home," said Mrs. Penhallow.

" You cannot understand," said I. " It does not seem to me as though Boston folks had any real home. Your houses are all just alike, and there are no trees and flowers and grass and a big piece of all out-of-doors for you."

" I do understand," she answered with unwonted gentleness. " Do you think that I can live, day after day, in my own lost home and not feel its influence? Morbid memories have kept Madam Penhallow's descendants from New Hampshire until now; but I have always felt towards it the genuine love for the fatherland. They say that nothing could keep Madam Penhallow long away from her home. I have always maintained that she and I had much in common."

"Don't say that, Sarah," remonstrated Mr. Penhallow. "The only resemblance between you is in your appearance."

"And that must have diminished if I am as ' peaked ' as Mrs. Wason says I am," she laughed. "See," holding out her left hand to me, "when I was married I insisted that my wedding-ring should be the same that the Penhallow women used to have — a bit of granite. It does not fit my finger as well as it once did."

"You must not stay longer in this damp place," urged her husband. "Sarah, don't!" For, as though in defiance of his words, she had sunk on her knees in the wet grass and was bending forward to scoop up some water with her hands.

"This is the way," I said, and pinned an oak leaf together in the form of a cup, which she filled and handed to Mr. Penhallow. She knelt till she had filled the cup again and satisfied her own thirst.

Harry had just turned into the driveway on

his return from his rounds as we approached the house again. The folks who now lived there were a young married couple, who made me free to come home whenever I pleased. The woman was standing in the doorway.

"We're jest a-settin' down to breakfus," said she, in greeting. "Hadn't yer better come in an' hev some? Yer must be hungry after yer ride."

"Let us go in, Mac. I want to breakfast in the queer little house," said Mrs. Penhallow, eagerly.

They insisted that I should have the place of honor at the table. Mrs. Penhallow ate heartily, and nobody would ever have known but that she was being entertained in the house of one of her own friends.

We finished the meal at last, and Harry went to unhitch the horse. Our hands were full of flowers as we again clambered to our seats in the wagon.

"We shall not forget our visit," called Mrs. Penhallow as we started down the steep driveway, our host and hostess smiling good-by to us from the doorway. "We will come again next summer and breakfast together."

But that never came to pass. When one day, the following year, I sat again as hostess in the little kitchen, two of those who had been with us on that sunny July morning had gone, never to return.

IX.

FOR the next few days Mrs. Penhallow was ill. The exposure in the wet grass, together with the jolting ride and the unaccustomed food at breakfast, combined to bring on a feverish condition, from which she was some time in rallying. The illness left its effect in neuralgic attacks that were sharper and more frequent than ever.

The ladies had been for some time past planning a hop. Caterers from Boston were to take charge, and Mrs. Wason had consented to let the old ball-room be restored, for that evening, to its original purpose. Mrs. Penhallow threw herself into every project, and was the acknowledged leader in all.

No one, however, knew the agony she endured, least of all her husband. In his presence all indication of pain was suppressed. I never knew how much of this concealment was due to the exercise of her will and the desire — that had its root mainly in a morbid fancy — always to appear her loveliest before him, and how much to a keenly susceptible nervous temperament, upon which excitement may have been a tonic more potent than quinine or aconite. But it was not worth while to play a part before me.

The folks were making a great ado decorating the ball-room. Mr. Wason drove some of them in his hay-cart to the woods, where they picnicked and remained till late in the afternoon, returning with a load of evergreen, boxberries, and ferns. The wash-tubs were to be filled with moss and young spruces, and the ironing-tables to be banked with flowers, for which the country around was scoured. Mrs. Penhallow was with the picnicking party, although she had been suffering terribly before she started. When I went to her room after her return, I found her kneeling by the side of the bed, her face buried in her outstretched arms.

"It is past help," she answered impatiently, when I wanted to summon the doctor. "It is intolerable. Life is not worth living at this price."

But when, half an hour later, the gong sounded and she came into the dining-room with her husband, there was not a trace of suffering on her face.

Nothing was talked about but the hop. There were a good many differences of opinion regarding the arrangements, out of which sprang much ill-feeling. One lady

wanted the hall draped with flags, and was
offended because somebody else said that it
was not to be a militia turn-out; and as the
first lady's husband was in the militia — she
always addressed him as " Colonel " — she
thought she was insulted, and would not
have anything more to do with the affair.
Then several of the young ladies arranged in
the corners bunches of cat-tails, tied up with
gay ribbons, and the children had a fine time
picking the down off the tails. Bits of fuzz
were all over the house and on everybody's
gowns for days after, and the ladies who had
children, and those who had not, were ranged
in opposing factions. Then some of the
ladies who had been gathering ferns took a
short cut home, with the result of losing their
way in a swamp; the next day most of their
number were afflicted with severe colds, and
were worried because they were afraid that
their eyes and noses would not be reduced in
time to their proper color and dimensions.
The cook scolded because all the sour milk
was used to anoint the burnt faces; Mr.
Wason grumbled because everybody expected him to be at beck and call, chopping
down trees and nailing up wreaths; and Mrs.
Wason declared a dozen times a day that it
was " pesky nonsense lit'rin' up the wash-
room with all that green truck."

Three or four days before the evening, Mr. Penhallow found it would be necessary for him to be absent a few days. As usual, Mrs. Penhallow begged him not to go. What did she care for the hop if he were not there? He tried to comfort her by pointing out that his absence could not have occurred at a better time than when she was engrossed with these multitudinous preparations, and promised that he would be back in time for the ball, even if he had to come by a special train. Her only reply was that she took no interest in anything if he was not by her side.

On the morning of his departure she had on a travelling-suit; I supposed that they had settled the vexed question by her accompanying him on his journey. But in half an hour there was a well-known peal of the bell. Mrs. Penhallow wanted some hot water. She had evidently been indulging in a good cry, her stratagem of keeping her husband company having failed.

The latest project in regard to the hop was to have it resemble the anniversary ball that had been given every year at the Place by Madam Penhallow. Even the date was to be the same. Then when somebody suggested that Mrs. Penhallow ought to play the part of lady of the manor, the idea was received with acclamation. But after this fresh impetus to the general interest there came a lull. The weather was hot, the mistress of ceremonies had evidently lost all interest in the affair, and the disappointments about the costumes were innumerable. The ladies who were so fortunate as to own old-fashioned gowns sent for them, Mrs. Penhallow being among the number; the others tried to borrow from friends, but with everybody out of town that was not an easy matter to arrange. Then there was another falling-out over the question, "Should masks be worn?" Those who had colds in their heads were loud in their favor, while the proposition was scouted by the ones who had escaped influenza. The decision finally reached was that everybody should suit herself, and go masked or not; with which settlement of the vexed question neither party was satisfied.

The day before the ball Mrs. Penhallow sent for me and showed me her gown; it was Madam Penhallow's own wedding-dress. "I take so little interest in the whole affair that I have only just unpacked this," she said. "If I had not agreed to play hostess, I would not appear at all. The lace is torn here and there — look at the frightful rent in the veil — and there is no time to send to Boston. Do you suppose you could mend it?"

My grandmother's instructions had been

thorough, but there proved to be more work than one pair of hands could accomplish alone. " If I might take it home, mother and I could work on it together," I suggested.

" Go at once, then," said Mrs. Penhallow; " I will speak to Mrs. Wason. You will not disappoint me? "

" I will bring it to you early to-morrow evening," I promised.

" The gloves, too, may need mending. I want to wear the whole costume," she added, and went to the bureau for the articles in question. With her impatient pull at the gloves, from out the confusion of the drawer a little round box fell to the floor and rolled to my feet. I picked it up and was about to replace it, when, to my surprise, Mrs. Penhallow snatched it from my hand. But not before I had seen the inscription on the label, below a little cut of a death's-head.

" Oh, don't! " I cried. " If you only knew " —

" If I only knew ! " she repeated, mockingly, in the high-pitched tones in which she had before given vent to her irritation. " What is the matter now? " she added abruptly, for at the familiarity of her unfamiliar voice my heart almost seemed to still its beating, my tongue had become dry and parched. I felt as though I were on the verge of a precipice, and then — the mist had shut out everything again. Instinctively I put out my hand like a blind person's.

Mrs. Penhallow went on, in calmer tones: " Are you going to preach the doctrine of milk and early to bed, too? I shall not die from morphine; they even say that the habit tends to prolong life — unfortunately, I often think, for I am growing more cadaverous and ugly every day." She pushed her hair from her face and regarded herself critically in the mirror. " ' Better be dead than ugly,' said Madame Récamier, and she was right."

In the morning I came over to the Place to assure her that my mother and I had already made considerable progress in repairing the lace. She was on the lounge in the dressing-room, white and spent with pain.

" I should not care if you were unable to finish the work," she said languidly; and then, talking more to herself than to me, she went on :

" I am fairly weighed down with a sense of impending evil. She drove her daughter Elizabeth to her death for having usurped her place in her husband's love. I have come into her home. I have slept beneath her roof, in her very room. I have usurped her name, her features, her character. To-night I am to take the final step."

There she was, running on again about ghosts and presentiments. I never stopped to draw breath till I was out of the house. I was so frightened and worried at her strange words that I repeated them to mother as we sat with our needles over the injured lace.

"Lor', child," said she, "that's dyspepsy. It's jes the way yer Aunt Elmiry takes on. Yer'd think as how she didn't calkerlate ter live another minute."

But my mind was not set at rest.

It was an intensely hot day, and every door and window was wide open. On the steps old Sally Waters sat, as usual, shrieking her terror. Of late she had been more restless and unmanageable than ever.

Our task was completed at dusk. Mother would return presently to fold the gown, in readiness for me to take to the Place; but now she must hurry to the dining-room, on the other side of the house, for there was to be blueberry pie for supper, and it would need all her authority to keep the paupers within bounds.

I hastened to my room. The maids were also to wear old-fashioned costumes, and my dress was one of my great-grandmother's — a bright figured muslin with the waist under the armpits. I spent a long time before the looking-glass, wondering how Harry would like me in my new-old array. I started at hearing the clock strike nine, for the dancing was to begin at that hour, and Mrs. Penhallow was without her gown.

In the entry below I ran into Harry's arms. " Aren't you coming ?" said he. " Oh, how nice you look! "

" Do you really like me ?" I asked.

" Like you! " he repeated, with emphasis. " There will be no one there who will look as nice. Come! They are marching around the room now. You never saw anything so splendid."

" What has Mrs. Penhallow done without her gown?" I exclaimed.

" Mrs. Penhallow has been there this half-hour at the head of the room."

Impatient at the delay, she had evidently sent for the dress, and mother must have given it to the messenger. A glance at the empty table where an hour before the robes had been outspread confirmed the surmise. So, gathering up my gown in one hand, I gave the other hand to Harry, and we raced up the hill and down again on the other side, and ran, breathless, up the piazza steps to ensconce ourselves near one of the long open windows, hidden from view behind the screen of metamorphosed wash-tubs.

X.

HER gown fitted Mrs. Penhallow as though it had been made for her. She wore no mask, but the heavy veil, drawn over her face, as effectively concealed her features. Mr. Penhallow was not present, and it was not difficult to understand why the hostess had elected to appear, after all, with masked face. She declined to dance, but moved about, at intervals, among her guests. Every one noticed how her head turned restlessly towards the entrance, and that her answers to any attempted conversation were singularly irrelevant. Naturally every one remarked:

" Mr. Penhallow will be here, I hope? "

" Yes, he is coming. He promised me that he would come," was the reply to all alike.

But the ten o'clock train arrived without bringing him. Mrs. Penhallow now seemed to avoid every one, and, as though her gloom were infectious, a chill had fallen upon the whole company. Harry and I could see how listlessly they moved through waltz and quadrille, and how they resolved into couples and groups as soon as each dance was at an end, keeping an anxious eye upon the door while they made pretence at conversation. Could any accident have happened to Mr. Penhallow? Their uneasiness, as well as mine, may have taken that form.

The whistle of the eleven o'clock train pierced the still summer night. Harry and I could see that somebody had stepped out at the station; that a man's figure was racing across the lawn, which, as it came within the radius of light from the portico, proved unmistakably to be that of Mr. Penhallow. We heard his footsteps upon the stairs and then the door of his room close. Supper was to be served at twelve o'clock, when the masks were to be removed.

There was a sudden stir in the ball-room, a cessation of the buzz of conversation, and a sigh of relief that was distinctly audible, coming, as it did, from all present, for the glances towards the door were at last rewarded. Mrs. Penhallow was hastening to meet her husband.

He was arrayed in knee-breeches and black silk stockings, with low shoes clasped by diamond buckles. With his ruffled shirt, the long lace ruffles that fell over his hands, the fair, curly wig with its cue tied up with a black ribbon, even his mustache gone that he might better play his part, he looked to perfection the gallant gentleman of the early century, and handsome enough to

5

have won any woman's heart. Husband and wife met by the window outside of which we stood.

She held out both her hands.

"I knew you would not fail me, Mac," she said softly.

"Not if human means could have prevented, darling. I was sorry that I could not get here before."

"The time has been long, love. And I was sorrowful, thinking of our parting. It was all my fault, Mac. I could not rest till I had begged for your forgiveness. I could not sleep, even in the grave, unless I knew that you had forgiven me."

"My darling, if all mortal sin were summed up against you, it would be outweighed by my love. I have wished more than once that I had answered you more gently, and had said good-by that last morning less abruptly. It was hard, love, to be left all alone in this great house."

"It was indeed empty without you."

"Not a moment has passed that I did not long to be at your side again."

"Kiss me, Mac."

"What — here? Before all these people?"

Accustomed as he was to her lofty disregard of comment, he was somewhat taken aback by this sudden demand.

"There is only one person in the room to me, but one to you."

He solved the dilemma by sinking on one knee and raising her hand to his lips. He retained the clasp as he arose.

"Your disguise is easily penetrated," he said gayly. "Your ring would tell tales, if nothing else did. I thought you were not to mask. There are those who need it more."

"But if I were one of those who wore a mask with cause, would you — love me less, Mac?"

"I cannot fancy you other than as you are."

But she pressed the question.

"You would care for me the same even though my beauty had become a thing of the past?"

"If I were absent a hundred years it could make no difference in my love, except to increase it a hundred fold."

The answer seemed to satisfy her.

"Let us stay here," she said softly. "I have not felt my hand in yours for so long."

Presently she saw me, in the dark, without.

"You are here, Martina?" she said. "You did well to have my gown in readiness; I could have worn nothing else."

Her voice, muffled though it was, sounded

sharper than its wont, except as I had
heard it in occasional moments of pain or
irritation, and the tones brought with them
the inexplicable weight of misery with which
they seemed always freighted. I had fancied
my uneasiness would be over with Mr. Penhallow's return.

The last waltz had come to an end. The
company were dispersed about the room,
waiting for Mr. and Mrs. Penhallow to lead
them to the supper-room. On a sudden
thought I ran around to the portico to see
the company march down the staircase.

The air was resonant with the hum of
voices and the softened strains of the band.
The leading couple were crossing the hall
below, when there suddenly appeared on the
threshold of the supper-room a familiar face
and form.

Was it a hideous dream? Were all in that
throng petrified in a nightmare, too, as they
gazed at the figure that was confronting the
stately couple who were leading the pageant?

It was Mrs. Penhallow.

There she stood, with one arm slightly up-
raised, and upon the third finger of its hand
there glittered the granite ring. Her white
gown clung to her like grave cerements.
Her face was pale and sunken and her eyes
were dimmed and heavy, wide open though

they were in their fierce, fixed gaze at that strange woman by her husband's side.

The silence was broken by a shriek, and then a long, piercing, blood-curdling wail:

" Elizabeth ! "

The figure that had borne its share in the evening's festivity had dropped the clutch on its companion's arm and darted through the open door into the darkness without. The heavy robes, the fluttering lace, brushed against me. The veil was torn aside.

And I saw what it had concealed.

Through the night, as the flying figure passed me, came the words:

" The witches are after me ! The witches are after me ! "

XI.

I ENTERED the poorhouse and staggered towards my mother's room. There was a light inside. At the sound of my voice my father came to the door.

" Where is she ? " I gasped.

"What does it mean ? " he questioned.

" Where is she ? " I repeated.

" Old Sally Waters roused us jes now by her shrieks at the door. How did she git hold of that dress ? "

"Where is she — where is she ? " I panted.

" Don't ask me anything now. Let me go to her; " and I freed myself from his grasp to hurry to the room at the end of the corridor.

There she lay on her bed of straw, the rich gown outspread in its length of train on the unpainted floor. Her staring eyeballs gleamed in ghastly unconsciousness through their half-closed lids.

My mother was trying to place a bedspread over her, but, as though she disdained the ugly calico coverlid, it was automatically pushed aside again and again. I sank on the chair by the bedside and buried my face in my hands. Mother and father stood by the door, whispering their conjectures. Once and again one of them would come to the bedside and scan the dying woman's face, but there seemed to be no change in her condition. Life was so plainly at its lowest ebb that it was not worth while to call the doctor.

On the floor near by was the leather string, knotted about a bit of gray flannel that the old woman had worn around her neck. I picked it up mechanically. In the rag a small circle was almost worn through, and in a cluster were two or three tiny holes. A few silky golden hairs clung to the rag.

The little blue chest at the head of the bed was open. Could the rags it contained, with

their loathsome contents, have been a tally by
which reckoning had been kept of the depart-
ing years? Had the sight of the wedding-
gown been the shock that had served to unite
old associations, and, sending all the life yet
left in the withered frame spinning and reeling
to the head, enabled the once iron will to make
its last mortal effort?

The minutes crept slowly on till that time
when death comes oftenest. The dying woman's eyes were suddenly opened. They met
mine. She raised her right hand and placed it
upon her left as it lay upon her breast, thus
covering the granite ring.

"I understand," I whispered.

A minute later the breathing ceased.

"Let her lie as she is," I said, when mother
would have disrobed her, "till I have told
Mrs. Penhallow."

Some boys were going past the poorhouse,
bound on an early fishing excursion. Their
mocking chant floated in to us:

> "Rise, Sally, rise,
> Wipe off your eyes!"

XII.

At the Place everything was in confusion. The halls were piled high with baggage, and ladies and children were standing about in travelling array. In the kitchen there was an excited group.

"Did you know — have you heard?" was the general exclamation as I entered. "Everybody is going, and Mrs. Wason is at her wits' end."

"Have the Penhallows gone?"

"They are going on the noon train. Most of the ladies fainted or had hysterics. One woman declared that she saw the figure whom we all thought was Mrs. Penhallow running over the hill towards the graveyard, and " — the girl lowered her voice and glanced nervously over her shoulder — "as true as you live, Mr. Wason found the veil this morning, as he was driving the cows to pasture, half way up the hill."

"Mrs. Wason says it was somebody playing a trick on us."

"It was Mrs. Penhallow or her double who was in the ball-room last night," cried another, argumentatively.

Without waiting to hear the end of the discussion, or rather its progress, for the end was never reached, I hastened to Mrs. Penhallow's room.

She was in bed, and her husband was seated near by, with an expression upon his face that would have been sternness in a less gentle nature. Here, too, I had evidently interrupted a discussion the nature of which was the same as that going on downstairs.

" Did you see it? " questioned Mrs. Penhallow, with a shudder.

I told them the inner meaning of the story which dated back eighty years. When I had ended, I was not crying alone.

" Let her be buried in her wedding gown," said Mrs. Penhallow ; " she will rest better so."

" You did not send for the dress, then ? " I asked.

" No. Soon after you left me I took some morphine. I had lately outgrown the influence of even largely increased quantities, and, indifferent to the risk of an overdose, I meant to take enough to insure escape from pain. Don't blame me too much, Mac. I have promised never to touch the horrible drug again. There was nobody to awake me through the day, for every one was resting in preparation for the evening. Even Mr. Penhallow's movements in the next room failed to arouse me.

"When I at last recovered consciousness my gown was damp with the dew from the open window. I was so dizzy and confused and so deathly sick that I did not realize what I had done or what was going on below. My only thought was that supper was ready and that I must hurry to meet Mr. Penhallow.

"Time seemed to have turned backward and I was the daughter whom the mother was driving to her death. The horror of the river to which she had at last succeeded in forcing me was upon me, my name rang in my ears, the phantasmagoria swam before my eyes, and that was all I knew till I awoke and found myself here."

By noon that day Penhallow Place was deserted, nor was there ever again any one bold enough to try the experiment of utilizing it as a hotel.

It was in the following spring that I wrote to Mrs. Penhallow about my marriage, and how Harry had said that it was on that morning in my old home when he had first thought how pleasant it would be always to sit at the table where I poured the tea.

In her reply she said that she was now in perfect health. Inclosed, a wedding present from her husband and herself, was the deed of the little rocky farm.

A MENTAL PRINCESS

I.

OLIVER DALLAS was coming over the ledges at full speed, jumping where he could not run, and now and again, at some "drop" in the path, catching hold of an overhanging branch and swinging himself down with an agility that would have done credit to an acrobat. He was singing at the top of his voice — not such a song as might have been expected from a Professor of Comparative Philology — a chant, for instance, of the chorus in "Antigone," as the play had been rendered last winter under his advice and supervision.

He was familiar with the Greek of Homer, the Sanskrit of the Vèdas, the Umbrian of the Inguevin Inscriptions; he could have given the different forms of a word in Sanskrit, Zend, Doric, Lithuanian, Old Slav, Latin, Gothic, and Armen, and its root in the mother Aryan. But by whom or at what era that verse he was singing was composed, he was as ignorant as the gamin whose rendering his trained memory had unconsciously jotted down:

Oh, Brian O'Lynn and his wife and his mother,
All went over the bridge together;
The bridge broke down and they all fell in.
"There's ground at the bottom," says Brian O'Lynn!

Perhaps the bracing air had acted as an intoxicant upon a system more than ordinarily sensitive; perhaps his youth was all at once asserting itself after having been held in abeyance for twenty-seven years, and, now that reaction had set in, carried him outside of the Oliver Dallas that the grave little world of professors and students knew. It would have failed to recognize even the outer man.

His coat showed the results of his scramble; the brim of his hat was rent from the crown, owing to the vigor with which it had been pulled over his head on the mountain-top; his face was unkempt with a three days' beard, and his inseparable eyeglasses were missing, having been caught in an overhanging branch that broke the bow, and he had no other pair nearer than the hotel, to which his portmanteau had been forwarded.

Some weeks ago, Dallas had been appointed delegate from his university to a convention of librarians. The honor was gratifying, but the pleasure small; for not only was the call an interruption of his work, but the convention was to be held, at the height of the season, at one of the large mountain hotels.

A hard student before he was out of petticoats, Dallas had given throughout his boyhood neither time nor thought to other pleasures than those afforded by his studies. At college the same course was pursued. A new language, particularly one so old that ordinary mortals did not even know of its fossil remains, had more charms for him than the various societies. While the men of his class were exciting themselves over some inter-collegiate boat race, he was poring over treatises and thumbing lexicons; the latest views in linguistics had more interest for him than the result of the last base-ball match. While still in his teens, he was a correspondent of noted specialists in philology, and had contributed articles on this subject to various German learned journals. He had lived so much, indeed, in the remote past that his ignorance of the present was as complete as might have been that of one of his beloved Aryans.

Although keeping aloof from athletics as an amusement, he had practised in the gymnasium with painstaking care, had never allowed work to interfere with sleep, and was as rigid in his diet as though under the most scientific training; so that he possessed the first requisite of the highest intellectual vigor, in being a good animal. His ignorance of the world, while it left him without much that was essential to a well-rounded development, had combined with the absolute healthfulness of his physical constitution to give him a purity of nature that made him shrink from all things mean or uncleanly with an intensity at times verging upon the finical.

He had reached the end of the woods, and, without warning, plunged headlong into a gathering of people. For an instant he stood dumbfounded.

Before him were several low, round tents. Two or three wagons stood near; groups of children were playing about; a youth was bringing an armful of sticks to a fire from which arose a smell of frying. A knot of women, engaged in basket-weaving, ceased their occupation to stare at the new-comer, who had dropped from the sky with loud words of ribald song; while several men in corduroy trowsers and red neckties turned toward him a scrutiny in which, if there was no welcome, there was yet nothing of enmity. A black hound, which had been dozing by the fire, gazed at him with the same expression of mingled suspicion and self-control that was in the faces of his masters.

"Sarishan!" called out the black-bearded stranger.

The faces of the men lighted up; the women began to buzz among themselves; the hound's head sank again upon his outstretched paws. One of the men stepped forward.

That his knowledge of Romany should ever be put to so practical a use had never entered into Oliver Dallas' most abstruse speculations. Interest in gypsies, as such, he had none. They were vagabonds, beggars, thieves; worst of all, they were dirty. But he could not be indifferent to the charms of a language still spoken, which was as old as Sanskrit, and probably older. There was a fascination which only a student of languages could understand in being able to study an ancient Hindu dialect in the very heart of modern civilization. Probably he not only spoke a purer Romany than the man with whom he was talking, but his vocabulary was actually larger.

With the same exhilaration that had flung him into the camp, he entered into the situation. There was no need for him to simulate; the rich physical life which had so long waited upon the mental was all at once dominant. He was a savage without the savagery, primeval man with a university record.

They asked him whence he came, not as people seeking credentials, but in friendliness and good-comradeship. He told them, without thought of prevarication, "from over there," with a jerk of his head towards the mountain. He was conscious that he was referring only to the last three days — that the years which had gone before were obliterated. He accepted their offer of food — he, who had as great a horror of pork as any Jew — and enjoyed the meal with the zest given by his long tramp. Afterward, while the men smoked and the women joined in the talk about the fire, he told stories and jested, as one who had passed his life beneath the "tan."

A girl sat by his side; in the gathering darkness and with his imperfect vision he could not discern her features, even though she had come gradually closer and he could now put out his hand and touch her. He did so, half unthinking, half because, in his keen enjoyment, he longed for the sympathy which comes with the magnetism of a hand-clasp. It did not surprise him that soft, warm fingers instantly closed upon his own. He was in the state of a man in a dream, in which the most extravagant situations and metamor-

phoses excite no wonder. So the twain sat
hand in hand, and the fire smouldered and
the stars were shining.

By and by, some one struck up a song and
the others joined in. It was such music as
Dallas had never before heard — melody to
which he could have listened, like the monk
of Hildesheim, thinking that three minutes
had passed, to awake and find that a thousand
years had flown. Then the voice of the girl
by his side took up the strain.

He would once have interpreted the story
of the Lorelei as a wind-myth. There crossed
his mind now, however, a wondering doubt
whether the tale of the magic power of a
woman's voice was not simple truth.

Half bewildered, half frightened, he strove
to cast off the spell.

He must go. He must be far from there
on the morrow — he scarcely knew what he
said, for the strains of the song were yet in
his ears — he groped, blindly, for their meaning — and the soft, clinging fingers had not
relaxed their hold.

Before he knew it, impelled by an irresistible power — partly, it may be, the result of
the intoxication of his senses, partly as the
culmination of that life-long reaction — he
whispered :

" *Miri pireni, me kamãva tut !* "

6

He spoke as the first of the race might have
done, unfettered by the rules and traditions
of society; free to follow the call of his own
nature; obeying blindly its impulse, unknow-
ing, unasking, and uncaring whence it came
or whither it would lead.   He heard, still as
in a dream, soft Romany words, with the
magic of the song lingering in their cadences:

*" Tu shan miro jivaben, me t'vel paller tute
— paller tute sarasa pardel puo te pãni !"*

II.

DALLAS awoke the next morning in his
hotel chamber with the words spoken in reply
to his own — *" My darling, I love you ! "* —
still ringing in his ears:

*" I will follow you wherever you go, over
land and sea, unto the uttermost ends of the
world !"*

Partly from his lifelong habit of weighing
and balancing language, of giving to every
word its exact value, as well as because he
had never spoken trifling words to a woman,
he felt as though he had pledged his soul to
some Mara, like the knight in the monkish
legend.

The gypsy girl had spoken those words as
though in earnest; and a whimsical thought

came to Dallas, from which he could not free himself, that she would reappear in pursuance of her vow at the very crisis of his life, and to his own undoing.

However, uncomfortable as the recollection made him, he could console himself with the thought that the convention would last only a few days, when he would depart by the next train for home and work, from out whose harborage he would never again venture.

He finished shaving and betook himself to the dining-room.

The breakfast gong had sounded some time before, but the apartment was still empty.

"They had a big hop here last night," said the waitress in an explanatory tone, as she led the way to his table. "It was after two o'clock when the folks went to bed, and I s'pose they're sleepy this morning."

Dallas had a vague recollection of a staircase with balusters wreathed with golden-rod, and of the sound of music issuing from some apartment that he had passed with hastened steps; but he supposed it was the usual state of things in a summer hotel, to be patiently endured unto the time of deliverance.

He looked about him. Garlands of evergreen were suspended across the ceiling, draped on the windows and drooped from the chandeliers; the one over his head, especially elaborate with great bunches of everlastings amongst the greenery, looked like a marriage-bell. Groves of young spruce were ranged along the walls. A litter of broken branches and pine needles had been swept aside and lay in fragrant heaps, to be removed at a more convenient season, and some of the curtains were still drawn.

The unreal appearance of a room in the morning light, after a festivity, added to the sense of strangeness that already burdened Dallas, and made him feel as though he was in an Arabian Night's tale, in which he was the only living person in an enchanted palace.

The door at the end of the hall opened. A girl was walking down the room with a firmness of tread and directness of purpose that was quite unlike the wobbly gait of the country maiden who had attended to his wants.

With a feeling akin to horror, he perceived that she was advancing toward the table where he sat — a feeling which reached its climax when the new-comer took a seat directly opposite him.

"Good morning, Mr. Dallas," said she. "You do not remember me?" as the young man failed to return the greeting.

"I do not," he made answer promptly.

There was no intentional discourtesy in
the disclaimer. Talleyrand to the contrary,
language was given to man to express his
thoughts. The girl laughed.

" Your tone says, ' Present your credentials ! ' I met you last winter at a rehearsal
of ' Antigone,' in the chorus of which I took
a distinguished part."

Dallas looked at her through his gold-
bowed spectacles much as he would have
scanned a word of whose root he was doubtful. His recollection of the Greek chorus
was merely of a medley of airy, iris-hued
draperies, in which personality bore no part.
The etymology of the young woman opposite
was not Greek. Her nose was irregular, her
face was browned by the August sun, her
light-brown hair was twisted into an unclassi-
cal knot on the top of her head; her gown,
too, — a trim, dark-blue skirt and jacket
braided with gold, — was quite unlike the
flowing draperies of a Greek maiden.

She was returning his scrutiny with a certain covert amusement that was not lost upon
its object; she had certainly the advantage in
knowing something of him. He felt that the
situation, beneath the marriage-bell, too, was
ridiculously connubial.

Were they the only two people awake in
the house? Would the waitress never re-

turn? In his embarrassment he was spelling out, letter by letter, the word " Terpsichore," printed in evergreens at the end of the hall.

" It should be — who was the Muse of Tragedy? — oh, yes, Melpomene," said his neighbor, with mock sympathy. " You make me feel so delightfully classical, Mr. Dallas. *De gustibus non est disputandum. E pluribus unum.* God bless our home! *Facilis descensus Averno* — with especial reference to our waitress. A week ago she attended to our wants fairly well. Crimps, a bang, German cologne, a reckless use of the opprobrious epithet ' lady,' have been the rapid stages of her descent. A Barmecide feast, is it not? Let me introduce our neighbors — by whom Love may be conjugated. This woman by my side is Love past. Love will henceforth be symbolized to my mind as a figure enveloped in a gray shawl and with a flannel compress around its throat. Love, instead of breaking Mrs. Hopkins' heart, has affected her larynx. On your right is Love present, Mr. and Mrs. Poole, a young bridal pair. Conversely to Hamerton's theory, that ' the mental prince should marry the mental princess,' the mental pauper has married the mental pauperess. Mr. Poole is teaching his bride geography and English history; but when he alluded the other morning to Marblehead's being on the Quincy branch, the shades of Radcliffe compelled me to refute the heresy. Consequently I am looked upon as one who scoffs at true love. Mr. and Mrs. Sillars, on your other side, present the picture of the sunny future. With her, love has developed into dyspepsia; with him, into a liver trouble. She spends her time in a haircloth rocking-chair in a corner of the sunless parlor, knitting bed-socks. He is devoting the summer to making a scrap-book of the criminal cases in the newspapers in which husband and wife figure. I suspect that one reason why love has waned in his case is that he reads poetry aloud whenever two or three are gathered together; and as the gypsies say, one must endure the chatter and say nothing " —

She cut herself short, for several other persons had entered the dining-room and were too near to make confidences longer safe.

" Strong tea, fried ham, hot biscuit, doughnuts, griddle-cakes and sirup — will somebody tell me why some people have everything in this world and I have not even health ? " come in lugubrious tones from Dallas' left.

" Gladstone, angel-pie," said a voice on the other side. " His first name is ' Premier.' "

Dallas looked across the table to meet his neighbor's eyes, with the malicious twinkle in their brown depths; and the look seemed to seal between them a sort of understanding, an undefinable feeling of good-fellowship.

A few hours later, Dallas attended the first meeting of the convention. As he stepped out on the piazza, still in grave discussion with one of his *confrères* on the copyright struggle in Congress, his ear caught words from a group of girls near by.

" The gypsies have gone! " one of them was saying.

" Gone! " came a chorus of dismay from the others.

" There is not a trace of them but the ashes of their fire."

There was an instant's hush, for Dallas had broken off his sentence midway and was evidently listening intently. Then, becoming conscious of his apparent rudeness, and recognizing his companion of the breakfast-table as one of the group, he bowed gravely and resumed his conversation. But it was no longer of international copyright that he was thinking.

The others had fallen away and he ventured near.

" The gypsies have been here? " he said interrogatively.

" An old woman came to the house yesterday to sell baskets," explained his morning's acquaintance, " and we planned to visit the camp this afternoon and have our fortunes told." She laid down her book, — a flimsy, paper-covered volume, — at which, because he did not know exactly what to say next, Dallas glanced, and read, besides the title, the name, in a free, bold handwriting, " Margaret Beach."

" Not that I believe in the gypsy method," pursued Miss Beach, gravely. " I insist upon my fortune being told according to the latest scientific light. None but Heron-Allen may look at my palm. Shall I read the future for you, Mr. Dallas ? "

The tips of her fingers touched, daintily, his own. What was there in the contact that nearly made him reel?

He was unused to the touch of a woman's hand, or — did the soft fingers bring back the moment when the ashes had been fire? For again those haunting, maddening words rang in his brain:

" *I will follow you wherever you go, over land and sea, unto the uttermost ends of the world!* "

Miss Beach was knitting her pretty, fair brows in profound study. Presently she spoke :

" The past is : You have played tennis a great deal. The future is : You are going to play, at once, — with me."

III.

IN the background of Dallas' life, where with other men had been youth, there was a figure lying on a sofa, with a novel in its hand, calling to everybody in weak, querulous tones, to do its bidding. Having seen how a nerve-vampire may suck the mental life out of a strong man, marriage meant to him merely exposure to interference, interruption, and ignorant criticism.

But here was a woman who was rejoicing in perfect health, yet who wore becoming gowns; who liked to dance; who read " Rudyard Kipling," — whoever he might be, — yet who could run without losing breath, and thought nothing of walking ten miles; who was not ignorant of Colebrook, Grimm, and Burnouf; who had a healthy appetite, and a waist that met the masculine approval, yet whose voice was even and controlled, and whose manners were gentle; who was at home in Egyptology, and still had an opinion of her own as to the merits of home-made yeast.

She aroused his curiosity as something new in his experience, then held his interest as the suggestion of future developments of the race, till, before he realized it, he was

talking to her as he had never talked to the
most congenial of his masculine associates,
under the stimulus of the intellectual com-
radeship of the woman that the last few
lustrums have developed. The convention
at an end, he made no secret to himself· of
the attraction which held him back from
home and his cherished studies.

With it all, he could not free himself from
a sense of moral incubus; and more than
once he awoke from a hideous dream — he
to whom a nightmare had been hitherto
unknown — in which a gigantic Mara was
pursuing him wherever he went, over land
and sea, unto the uttermost ends of the
world, while a voice that sounded like his
own was repeating again and again:

"*Miri pireni, me kamãva tut!*"

How she would scorn him if she knew —
she, who from the very beginning of their
acquaintance had lost no opportunity of
scoffing at love!

And there was no doubt but that love was
fast becoming obsolete. Admirable as a
provisional arrangement for the continuance
of the race, as the growth and demands of
the intellectual life increased, "the silly,
senseless, and savage element" dwelt upon
by Max Müller was becoming happily elimi-
nated from the social arrangement no less

than from religion. In the future, natural selection would mean that "the mental prince would marry the mental princess."

Were confirmation needful of his theory, how could that be worthy whose lees, as with Mrs. Hopkins, had soured life, making her every utterance censorious? Could there be aught ennobling in a feeling which had drawn together two such people as Mr. and Mrs. Poole? Upon such a foundation, the marriage of Mr. and Mrs. Sillars had resulted in mutual misery. Moreover, when he asked Miss Beach to marry him, no moonlit balcony, with its attendant influenza and rheumatism, should be the scene of a proposal dictated by healthy reason, but the hotel parlor, in broad daylight, after dinner.

It was that evening that Miss Beach was asked to sing. She complied, with Bourdillon's verses:

> The night has a thousand eyes
>   And the day but one;
> Yet the light of the bright world dies
>   With the dying sun.
>
> The mind has a thousand eyes
>   And the heart but one;
> Yet the light of a whole life dies
>   When love is done.

Beyond criticism in technique the rendering was without feeling or expression.

" He sang only that one song," commented Miss Beach as she arose, "and the reason was that he was struck dumb afterward, like Ananias."

Mr. Sillars, perhaps impelled by a morbid desire to make others as unhappy as himself, had begun to read "Tam o' Shanter," in a droning, mouthing utterance, with the evident intention of keeping on to the bitter end. Mrs. Sillars gathered up her knitting and fled. Mrs. Hopkins drew her shawl more closely about her, and, murmuring something about "my poor throat," glided from the room. Mr. and Mrs. Poole remembered, simultaneously, that they had a letter to write. Miss Beach suggested that the air on the piazza was fresher than in the parlor, and Mr. Dallas agreed with her.

He noticed how pretty his companion looked in the moonlight, with a satisfaction which sprang entirely from self-complacency that his pulse was beating as calmly as ever. They sat in silence for some minutes; and that, too, pleased Dallas, because intellectual companionship does not demand the incessant chatter requisite to the contentment of the young bridal pair. After all, there might be no better opportunity than the present.

Without unnecessary circumlocution or foolish hesitation, he began :

" I doubt if there is such a thing as love
amongst the educated classes. As Spencer
suggests of remorse, I am convinced that
it figures merely in novels or upon the
stage."

" I agree with you," answered Miss Beach,
promptly.

" A marriage based upon a calm con-
sideration and comparison of the characters
and tastes of the parties concerned, is the
only one to be recognized after man has
outgrown the instincts he shares with the
animals."

" You are quite right," returned his companion calmly.

" And so you will marry me ? "

The children were playing " Blind-man's-
buff" in a room near by; they were drawing
lots for " Blind-man " by means of a familiar
nonsense verse. With an interest painful in its
intensity, Dallas listened to the meaningless
jingle, awaiting breathlessly some unknown
but terrible issue when that last syllable
should have fallen upon him.

" Stingle 'em — stangle 'em — buck ! " came
in a crescendo of childish voices.

" No ! " almost shrieked Miss Beach.

Before he could find voice, her hand had

spasmodically grasped his own, and she demanded, fiercely:

" Do you hear that? "

The children had begun the chant again:

> One-eri — two-eri — ekkeri — an —
> Fillisi — follasy — Nicolas — jan —
> Queebee — quabee — Irishman,
> Stingle 'em — stangle 'em — buck!

" Do you know what it means? "

" They are Romany words, curiously pre-
served, almost uncorrupted, in children's
games," explained Dallas, professional instincts conquering. " They mean —

> First — second — here — you begin —
> Castle — gloves — you don't play — go on " —

" I don't care what they mean," interrupted
his companion wildly, " except that they are
gypsy! People talk about the power of drink
or opium — what is it, compared to the spell
of a gypsy word! I don't know how or when
it began. I suppose there must be gypsy
blood in my veins, too far back to be traced.
My old nurse used to explain it otherwise.
But — atavism or ' a little divil inside o' me '
— it is there! I gave my pennies, before I
could talk plain, to an old scissors-grinder, to
teach me Romany. The sound of a gypsy
word, the sight of a gypsy face, sets my blood

on fire. What did I care for the hop of the season if I could sit for an hour by a gypsy camp-fire!

"It was then *he* came. I sang to him. Not as I sang to-night, but so that he understood and answered, not in cold, measured terms of hateful reason, but in words that have rung in my ears, day and night, ever since.

"I shall never marry. I dare not! For if he should speak those words again I should leave all — friends, home, husband — and follow him wherever he went, over land and sea, unto the uttermost ends of the world!"

His hand had closed on hers in a clasp that may, of itself, have brought recollection; and he whispered:

"*Miri pireni, me kamāva tut!*"

A RETURN TO NATURE

" REV. AUGUSTINE ST. GREGORY, Miss
Helen Mackintosh. Married" —
" Tear up the wedding-cards ! " interrupted
Pris Armstrong. " It was infatuation — fa-
naticism. How could a Boston girl, brought
up with every advantage of education and
association, marry a full-blooded Sioux! I
went to the wedding under protest; as
Helen's nearest friend, I sat there under
protest; and it required all my self-control
to refrain from shrieking aloud at the words:
' If any man can show just cause why they
should not lawfully be joined together' " —
" You talk as though he had just arrived
from the plains, in wampum and war-paint,"
returned Annie Chesley, indignantly. " I
met him at Mrs. Cotting's reception, and
thought him perfectly fascinating. He has the
loveliest manners — so gentle and subdued,
and, with his soulful dark eyes and melancholy face, he reminded me of Edwin Booth
in 'The Iron Chest.' Such an interesting

7

history as he has, too! He lost his father at
the battle of the Little Big Horn, and after
the flight of Sitting Bull and his men into
Canada, the poor little fellow was found by a
missionary and sent to Hampton. Later, by
means of an old lady's bequest, he was
educated for the ministry, preparatory to
going as missionary to his own people. If
you had heard him speak, the last Sunday in
Advent, when the collection was taken for the
Domestic Missions, you would realize what
religion has done in transforming a savage
into a Christian gentleman and clergyman."

" Helen was taught from babyhood to save
her pennies for the Domestic Missions," said
Pris, slowly. "In Lent her childish sacri-
fices were for the benefit of some Indian
school. Her cast-off toys were sent to
Hampton; her Sunday-school class supported
an Indian there. Later she attended all the
meetings for the benefit of the Indians, has
been an active member of the Dakota League,
and devoted all her charitable energies —
and a Boston girl must have some outlet for
her inborn spirit of philanthropy as impera-
tively as for her love of music, books, and
art — to collecting funds and packing barrels
of clothing for the Indians. As she stood by
the altar, it seemed the culmination of a
lifelong fad, — an earnest and religious one,

if you will, but still merely a fad, — in which love bore a minor, if not a doubtful, part. There was a delay in getting to the carriage, and I waited on the curbstone. No, not to throw rice, but — but to see Helen once more. Captain Carter, Helen's cousin, — he was best man, — closed the carriage door, with a gay good-by. He stood with uncovered head in the fog and drizzle, and I saw the look upon his face."

" They say he has always been in love with Helen."

" It was not that. Insight gave foresight, and on the pavement in Copley square he saw the future, somewhere on the Western plains."

.   .   .   .

" You are tired, August?"

Helen St. Gregory arose from the piano, — the one article of luxury she had permitted herself, — and, leaning over the back of her husband's chair, played with his hair. It had been allowed to grow somewhat long in the last few weeks.

He had just returned from a visit to a settlement a few miles distant, consisting of a few wretched, scattered huts. His hand sought his throat and loosened the stiff clerical bands with an impatience that seemed uncontrollable.

"It is stifling here," he said; "the air of a room makes me cough."

"I will open the window."

"Open both windows!"

"I cannot," returned Helen, with some surprise at his imperious tone. "The other window is sealed hermetically with *papier-maché* manufactured out of soaked news-papers, after Frank Carter's recipe."

Her husband strode across the room, and with one blow of his clenched fist broke away the lower part of the sash.

"August! How could you — Oh, your hand is bleeding!" reproach changing to commiseration.

She caught up a web of soft linen upon the work-table.

"It is nothing," said her husband almost haughtily, drawing himself so quickly away that the linen fell beneath his foot.

The next moment there was an exclamation from both, for it was the surplice, with the circle-emblem of immortality embroidered upon its front, that lay there, blood-stained and trampled.

He sank into the chair again, and she, who had learned in the last few months that there were times when it was best to leave him undisturbed, silently closed the shutters outside the broken window and pinned closely over it the heavy curtains of Mexican blankets. The room was both sitting-room and study. In the corner a *prie-dieu*, with a threadbare cushion, testified to the length and frequency of his devotions.

Presently Helen looked anxiously up from the altar-cloth she was embroidering.

"I wish you would not watch me in that covert manner," said her husband, with new irritability.

He was tired, she thought, and her woman's heart chid her for a moment of strange and chilled misgiving. It was a long, cold walk to the settlement, and the people there were the most degraded of his pastoral charge. They consisted only of old men, women, and children; the young men were out hunting — a euphemism for having joined certain hostile tribes in the North-west.

"I have questioned lately, Helen," he began presently, "whether I have not, after all, mistaken my vocation. The fire has died out of my utterances; my prayers no longer ascend as on wings of light, but fall crushingly back upon my heart. The meaning has gone out of the Holy Scripture; its words are as 'a tale told by an idiot, full of sound and fury, signifying nothing.'"

She spoke gentle, reassuring words, but

the strange foreboding returned, and bided in her heart. Long after she had gone to bed, he was kneeling at the *prie-dieu*.

In the days that followed, she noticed that he was unusually silent; that the early services, the prayers, and fastings became more frequent — the last so rigorous that she begged him to have care lest his health suffer.

"We are commanded," he replied solemnly, "to 'crucify the old man and utterly abolish the whole body of sin.'"

He went about his work like a man in a dream. The melancholy that had always characterized him became moodiness, a taciturnity that his wife learned was best left unquestioned. His favorite subjects of conversation had formerly related to his work; now he never alluded to it. His texts had been chosen from the New Testament, that upon which he had most frequently dwelt being, "For their sakes I sanctify myself, that they also may be sanctified through the truth." Now his sermons were drawn from the Old Testament, and particularly from those accounts that dwelt upon vengeance and bloodshed. When he read the lesson telling of the killing of Sisera, there was a repressed force in his utterance, an intensity of dramatic action in the gestures of his slender hand and flexible wrist, that brought the scene with awful vividness before his listeners.

"She smote the nail into his temples — for he was fast asleep and weary. So he died." His personality was merged into that of Jael, and exaltation was exultation over the treacherous and savage deed.

His manner in speaking of his own people had formerly been tinged with sadness. Was it a wild fancy of his wife's that it now held a subtle pride? A distinction, too, had evidently grown up in his mind between "these people" — the reclaimed sheep of his flock — and those amongst whom his childhood had been passed.

His walks over the plain became more frequent. Helen had supposed their object was the settlement, till an allusion to his work there undeceived her. "I have not been there. I walked twenty, thirty miles over the plain," he said, with an excitement that all her efforts at restraint could not ignore.

"Listen!" and the words that followed were strange to Helen. "It is the tongue of my fathers," went on her husband, with solemn pride. "Upon the vast empty plain there was a sound from heaven as of a mighty rushing wind, and even as the tongues were given to the disciples at the

day of Pentecost was the language of the
warriors given back to me. With such
words did my father speak when he told of
his deeds at the council fire. My father was
a great brave. He did not live amongst the
women and children. He was not a squaw-
man. He was Black Kettle!"

Bewildered at this strange outburst, Helen
called beseechingly to her husband. He
made no reply. It was morning when he
arose from the *prie-dieu*.

For the next few days, except for an
almost unbroken silence, he seemed more
like his former self. Late one afternoon, in
his absence, word was brought to Helen that
a woman had been confined in the settlement,
and was dying for lack of proper care, food,
and clothing. The circumstances of the case
appealed to her with peculiar force. Filling
a basket with food, and hastily selecting such
articles as seemed most needful, she set out
on her lonely walk.

The door of the hut was ajar. Its one
room was empty. In her charitable visiting
in Boston a similar experience had often
been hers, and now, as then, an involuntary
vexation arose at having been made the
dupe of her sympathies. She made her way
to the next hut, but, to her surprise, it, too,
was empty. She walked on, thinking to

find some one to question, but the search was vain. The village was deserted!

The last hut stood on the brow of an incline. In the hollow beyond was a strange sight.

Shrinking back into the shadow of the hut, petrified with horror, she stood watching a circle of savage figures, men and women alternating, holding one another by the hand, revolving slowly around a large tree. A dirge-like chant filled the air, as round and round the dancers went, in the same direction, with eyes closed and heads bent toward the ground. There were young men in the circle. Had they returned, then, from their " hunting expedition "?

Chained to the spot by the mystic spell of the " ghost-dance," her own body swayed to and fro in unison with the dancers.

One figure seemed to exercise a particular fascination over her. It was that of a young brave, naked to the hips, and with streaks of red and yellow paint across his breast. Darkness had long ago fallen, and fires were gleaming in the hollow, but still Helen watched, spellbound. One after another of the dancers fell forward on his face in a kind of swoon, but the circle was instantly re-formed. The young brave who had held her gaze was prostrate at last.

Suddenly he leaped to his feet.

" I have seen the Great Father," he cried, " and he will not talk to me because I have married a white woman ! "

It was the voice of her husband !

Half-frozen, blinded, and staggering, Helen reached her own door at last. She must have wandered many times from the path, for the cold, gray morning light was breaking. She dropped, from force of habit, into the chair by the work-table. She must darn those socks of August's. It was the morning for early service. She took up a little illuminated book of devotions in which it was her daily habit to read. Was she going mad? The words were revolving in a circle over the page. A capital *A*, in scarlet and gold, bore a fantastic resemblance to the paint-bedizened figure of the dance.

There was a sound without. The door was pushed open and a naked savage strode into the room. She saw his purpose.

" August ! For the sake of our unborn babe ! "

What followed may not be told.

THE TENTH OF SEPTEMBER

WHAT I am about to relate is no mere ghost story — would to God it were! No breath of icy air, chilling my very marrow, no footfall, as of "Silence, step by step increased," no rustle of impalpable garments, has it ever been my fate to know. To see or hear, whatever of the unimaginable might be revealed, would be freedom.

It may have chanced that alone at midnight, after hours of concentrated toil, you are leaving the darkened room, when you have been stricken with a sudden unreasoning horror of something, you know not what, that was striving to grasp you from out the emptiness behind. On waking from deep sleep there has loomed before your straining eyes a horrible, impalpable shape that yet was no shape, but the very darkness endowed with a malignant life. Of something that nature, increased indefinite fold, is the Presence that has made existence to me a curse.

Since the days of our ancestor, the second

governor of the Massachusetts Bay Colony, our family had followed one profession, — that of physician. When the era of specialty dawned, my grandfather adopted that of Neurology; my father made the same choice; and, from my earliest recollections, it was understood that I was to follow in their footsteps. After taking my Harvard degree, I studied for several years at Edinburgh and in Germany, and returned to Boston to step into a lofty and assured position in my chosen calling. Besides assisting my father in his numerous private cases, — he deferred to me if our diagnoses conflicted, — I was a member of the Visiting Board of two asylums for the insane, was appointed lecturer on Neurology at the Medical School, and published a book, "Responsibility in Mental Disease," that was quoted by those who were themselves authorities.

While I supposed that the world held nothing for me but my profession, I met Helena Kay. There may have been girls that were prettier, more accomplished, more attractive in the general sense, but none whom I had ever met fulfilled my ideal of womanhood till I knew Helena. Neither her nature nor mine was of the kind that " falls " in love, but one day we awoke to the full and blissful assurance that we loved each other

as man and wife should love. Congratulations poured upon us; we were of the same
rank in life, and people said we "fitted."
My father's beatitude as he welcomed his
"daughter" was complete.

To be worthy of Helena I worked harder
than ever to win a loftier name, a wider fame,
in my calling. In the preparation of an ex-
tended work on the "Hallucinations of Insanity," it became desirable to consult several
eminent men in England, and to visit some
of the hospitals for the insane on the Conti-
nent. Accordingly, I decided to spend the
ensuing months abroad, returning immediately before the third of October — our wedding day. In September, after a season of
intense mental activity, I found myself in
London. On the evening of the tenth, Sir
James Gordon, the eminent surgeon, gave a
farewell dinner in my honor. Nothing of an
exciting nature had occurred during the day.
The conversation at the table was upon com-
monplace topics. At no time was it my
habit to exceed one glass of wine *per diem*,
and that night a single sip of sherry was all
that had passed my lips. The dinner had
reached saddle of mutton when suddenly I
became aware of the awful Presence that will
never leave me this side the grave.

Starting from my chair, I glanced fearfully

over my shoulder. With a face frozen with horror, I looked into every corner of the brilliantly lighted room. Instinctively I grasped the human hand of my neighbor; the contact revealed mine cold as ice. Twice, thrice, I tried to speak, but my lips were stricken with dumbness.

The buzz of conversation had suddenly ceased, and every one at the table was staring at me.

"For God's sake, Dudley, what has happened?" cried my host.

I seized the decanter, poured out and drank, in rapid succession, three, four glasses of sherry, and looked around on the circle of anxious, mystified faces like one awakening from a swoon. Solicitations were poured forth, questions heaped upon me, but, with pallid face and icy hands, I kept my secret, as I have guarded it from that hour to this. Who, indeed, of all the world, could understand the horror that had befallen me? Dinner was soon at an end. Disguise it as they would, not a man but what was anxious to flee my presence.

The tenth of September! Then was drawn the dividing line between me and humanity.

It was only in the first days of my possession that I attempted to analyze the nature of that mysterious Presence; afterwards, I

might as well have attempted to analyze my
own soul. It seemed to me conceivable that
with the cumulative effect of generations
devoted to one line of thought, — and that
dealing almost exclusively with mental con-
ditions, — increased possibly in my own case
by some special individual aptitude, my
intellectual faculties had outstripped their
proper balance with the physical, till a state
was reached in which the mental perceptions
acted without the aid or intervention of the
bodily senses; that the inward vision, thus
magnified, had obtained cognizance of some
Reality in the psychical world that was none
the less real, because not reducible to for-
mulæ.   Could Coleridge have had a similar
experience and so made it the animus of the
Ancient Mariner, shunned by all men? What
mysteries had been unveiled to Keats before
he wrote his terrible " Lamia "?

Concomitant with Its presence, I was aware
of what I can only describe as a kind of
double consciousness.   One was that of my
real self, whose keynote was Helena; the
other part of this dual nature was under some
dominant influence that controlled not only
my acts, but my very thoughts and passions.
A sensation somewhat akin to this strange
mental state occasionally occurs in sleep,
when, all moral feeling at an end, one com-

mits the most atrocious crimes with indiffer-
ence, yet with the cognizance, underlying
subconsciousness, that these horrors are a
dream from which presently he will awake
and all will be well. But, fettered as in a
nightmare, I knew that when I awoke I
should find that the acts and penalties of my
dream were real.

Leaving London without farewells, I
hastened to Liverpool, where I was unknown,
and for three days and nights struggled in
the spiritual torment of Laocoön; but the
coils grew ever closer and tighter, and my
power of resistance weakened hourly. I had
gone early on board the boat, and stood by
the rail on the upper deck moodily watching
the stream of people pass over the gangway,
when my glance fell upon a young girl; she
was chatting and laughing with a group of
acquaintances, whose hands were filled with
farewell tributes of flowers and boxes of bon-
bons. There was nothing in her appearance
to which positive exception could be taken;
only, to a critical eye, the impression it conveyed was that of one just below the social
line; scarcely vulgar — not high-bred.

Attracted by my fervent gaze, she glanced
upward and our eyes met. Eagerly I awaited
her reappearance on deck; as she came in
sight, my heart beat madly, and, forgetting

home, Helena, the third of October, I started forward, intent on I know not what. At that moment a young man belonging to the travelling party, who was apparently acting as the girl's special escort, placed his hand upon her arm, and the familiarity maddened me with what I dared not call jealousy. At that moment a lady near me caught a glimpse of my face, and, with an involuntary exclamation, hurried from my neighborhood, casting an affrighted backward glance.

That night, sleeping or waking, a pink and white face was ever before me. I did not seek to disguise from myself the motive that took me early on deck the next morning. Presently she — the girl for whom I waited — appeared, and passed me with a smile that was easy to interpret. My unreproved greeting was followed by a light, flattering speech, at which she dimpled bewitchingly; then, with studied but palpable hesitation, she accepted my invitation to walk the deck, and presently acceded to a petition to be allowed to place her chair and arrange her rugs. The morning passed in the secluded corner.

Every moment of the ensuing days I was at her side. The passengers smiled significantly at our mutual absorption, and even made opportunities for us to be together, after the usual temper of people toward acknowledged lovers. On the third day out I asked her to be my wife — and all the while my other self was conscious of Helena.

We were married in New York the day of our arrival, and took the train immediately for Boston, her home as well as mine. With supreme disregard for consequences, I gave orders to drive to my father's house; leaving Mabel in the reception-room, I entered the study unannounced.

"My boy!" exclaimed my father, holding out his hands, his fine face aglow. "Here is one who will rejoice even more than I," he added, turning to Helena, who stood before me silent, but with shining eyes and happy, curved lips.

I awoke!

In the overwhelming tide of feeling that bore down upon me, I staggered, and sank into the nearest chair. One lightning flash appeared out of the blackness of darkness. I had lost Helena!

"He is ill, poor boy, as we feared when we received no telegram," said my father. "There was a look in his eyes as he entered that I did not like."

Helena's cool, soft hand was placed upon my forehead. The touch brought sickeningly home my treachery.

"Don't touch me!" I cried, as a leper of

old might have called out his woful warning,
" Unclean ! " " I am married ! "

" A touch of delirium," said my father,
professionally. "We must get him to bed;
overwork " —

" Don't you understand? " I repeated,
irritably; "I tell you I am married. My wife
is with me."

Helen's arm slipped around my neck.
There was no trace of foolish embarrassment
in her voice or manner as she bowed her
head and whispered, so that only I could
hear: "Yes, my own, I am with you,
always. I will never leave you."

The door was pushed abruptly open and
Mabel entered. For a few moments there was
silence. Then my father spoke, calmly and
icily, " This room is no place for you,
Helena. Will you take my arm? "

Presently he returned.

" Now, sir, what is the meaning of this? "
he demanded sternly.

In silence, I handed him the marriage cer-
tificate. He was long in reading the few
lines.

" The old gentleman doesn't seem exactly
glib with his congratulations," suggested
Mabel, even her self-assurance shaken by this
reception. " I thought it was time I put in
an appearance," she added, in a strident

whisper. " I was at the door, you know; naturally, I felt an interest in what was going on."

Utilizing the glass door of the adjacent bookcase as a mirror, she pulled out her frizzes and settled her neckgear to her fancy. Then, her equanimity apparently restored by the pleasing reflection, she turned to my father.

" We've taken you by surprise, I suppose," she simpered. "George couldn't wait for even a wedding-gown, though I've always said " —

" Never let me see you again," said my father, pointedly addressing me, and motioned to the door.

" Aren't we going to live here?" queried Mabel, in a loud, aggressive tone. " I won't stir a step from this house. I've ordered our ' At Home ' cards" —

"Come," I said sullenly; and for once silenced, she followed, and we left the house.

My wife's people lived on an avenue that, having attempted fashion and achieved vulgarity, sank, by a natural transition, to the unmentionable. A house here and there retained something of its former comparatively decent estate, and in one of these florid, arrogant dwellings, that one instinctively felt was besmirched without and within by its surroundings, Mabel's parents received me, at first with flattery, changed by rapid degrees to questioning looks and unconcealed ill-feeling, as, day by day, the mistake their daughter had made grew more evident.

Having, from habit of life and from well-justified confidence in my own ability to command an income commensurate with my tastes, always lived to the extent of my professional earnings, I had no money laid by. Financial straits were soon added to my misery. With that exaggerated class feeling inherent in the "Brahmin caste" of New England, the people amongst whom my private practice had laid, for the alleged reason of my treatment of one of their number, no longer sought my advice. I received a courteous intimation from the Medical School that the course of lectures which I had been invited to deliver had been abandoned, for reasons, etc. My position on managerial boards became so unpleasant that I proffered a resignation that was accepted without mention of "reconsideration."

Accompanying and accentuating this tangible trouble was the awful, unknowable Presence that at times seemed to be driving me mad. I might, indeed, have suspected my sanity, had it not been that during the entire period of my possession my mental faculties remained unclouded; in fact, day by day, my intellect seemed to grow clearer, more luminous. Besides, would not I, a recognized authority on Neurology, have been the first to recognize a morbid disturbance of my own nervous system?

Sometimes It would leave me free for days. Then the sudden consciousness of Its presence would overwhelm me, with Its concomitant sense of double consciousness. It did not always *dominate;* that phase apparently asserted itself in the more important junctures of my life, leaving me free in the mere details of every-day intercourse; but the *Presence* came and went erratically — at wakeful midnight, as I bought a paper of a newsboy, or walked the crowded street at noonday. However dense the throng, I was never trodden by careless foot nor jostled by heedless elbow.

One day, as I put the latch-key into the door of what I called my home, It was suddenly with me. Mabel was in the parlor with the young man who had been her companion that first day on the steamer. His name was Fred Martin. I did not love my wife. I did not even hate her. I knew I had no cause for jealousy. But as I saw her and Martin seated familiarly side by side, a mad passion of anger and hatred took possession of me.

Involuntarily glancing up at the sudden shadow in the doorway, Mabel's sudden start was evidence of guilt. At the expression of my face, she pressed closer to Martin, and clasping his arm with both hands, cried, beseechingly:

" Fred, Fred, don't let him hurt me. I am afraid ! " and burst into hysterical sobs.

The disturbance brought her father and mother to the room. Mabel was soothed and petted, apologies were offered to Martin, I was told, in undisguised language, that I was a monster. Scant, indeed, was the tolerance now meted out to me !

This episode ushered in a new state of affairs. Mabel could not leave the house that I did not dog her footsteps. I ransacked her desk, her bureau, for guilty correspondence. Martin was an old friend, nothing more. I drove her into her sin, if, indeed, sin it was. Partly from the comfort his sympathy gave, partly because of my opposition, for Mabel — I write it without reproach — was of that nature that delights in the forbidden, what my jealousy, that was yet not *my* jealousy, feared, came to pass. One day my wife wore a little bunch of violets at her breast. I tore the flowers from her and, like a raging beast, trampled them under foot. " As I would do to him ! " I muttered.

My wife did not, as usual, have recourse to tears.

"Why did you marry me, if only to treat me so!" she cried. "And I—what a fool I was! I thought it would be fine to have my cards engraved 'Beacon street,' but much good your name or money has done me. I wish to heaven I had married Fred Martin, and let you keep your engagement to Miss Kay!"

"Did you know that I was betrothed?" I demanded, holding her by the wrist as she would have left the room.

"Of course I did," she answered, fear forgotten in anger. "Don't you think that I had read the passenger list and knew you for a howling swell before I came on deck. Do you take me for a fool?"

"I take you for something worse," I began recklessly, when she snatched herself away and hurried from the room casting a backward look of scorn and hatred. Heaven help me — if Heaven there be! — I deserved both.

After hours of aimless wandering through the streets, I returned to find that my wife had left me, with Martin. Her father awaited me.

"There is but one course open," he said sternly. "She must be set free to marry Martin. Before Heaven, she is blameless, but the plea for divorce must come from you."

"I have no money to purchase my wife's virtue," I returned doggedly, "low as the market price appears to be."

Her father made a gesture of impatience.

"You shall have all the money that is necessary. It is not by your treatment of my daughter," he went on, in another tone, — a tone from which natural resentment had died, — "that you have inspired me with a feeling unlike mortal hatred, the like of which I have never known before, and which, I pray to God, I may never know again. I say to you, without passion, that I would rather my only child should live as Martin's mistress than as your wife!"

So, at my instance, a suit for divorce was entered. The newspapers printed daily bulletins of its progress, with the customary illustrations. One cut represented me dragging my wife about by her hair, on her refusal to partake of the bottle labelled " Poison " which I was somewhat indiscreetly brandishing. Everything was against me. I attempted no defence. Mabel shone out an afflicted angel of light and goodness. The divorce was granted, and, in due time, Mabel married Fred Martin.

I hired an attic room in the labyrinth of

lanes at the South End whose very existence is unsuspected by the well to do and respectable, and picked up a precarious living by those methods damned in the word — *unprofessional.*

In one of the long, rambling walks in which, goaded like Orestes of old, my nights were frequently passed, I started to discover that my unwitting footsteps had led me to the neighborhood of my former home. The street was thickly strewn with tan. The precaution could only mean that my father was very ill. I knew his malady — the sight of his old and honorable name dragged through the mire. The longing to see him, if only once again, took possession of me, and, without giving myself time for reflection, I mounted the familiar steps and pressed the bell. No sound followed, but a servant evidently on guard in the hall opened the door.

"Let me in; I wish to see my father," I said imperiously, and without allowing time for denial or parley, pushed past the bewildered man and made my way up the stairs and into my father's room.

Dr. Fredericks, an old friend and professional colleague of my father, was seated at the bedside. He frowned at my entrance, then arose and beckoned me into the hall.

" Is he dying? " I questioned hoarsely.

" To-night will decide," answered the doctor, with stern brevity. " For what have you come? "

"To see my father," I answered humbly. " For what else could I have come? I knew but just now of his illness. For God's sake, don't keep me from him ! "

Dr. Fredericks' fine-featured face, at first unrelenting, grew troubled, then perplexed. Finally, the old physician said solemnly, " It may be that your footsteps were guided to this hour ! Your father will probably have a moment of consciousness toward midnight," he went on. " I dare not leave a dying man — for there is scant hope — with a possible longing ungratified, nor you without the chance for forgiveness of which of all living men I earnestly believe you stand most in need. You were once the worthy son of your father, George Dudley. And my pride in your achievements was scarcely less than his. In your hands I leave him. And pray to God," he added, lifting his hand in the inspiration of that moment when the ordained physician feels himself the Great High-Priest of the Almighty, " that in His great mercy He may grant you opportunity to win back the life that you, and you only, have brought to this pass."

I bowed my head and reëntered the sick-room.

The nurse was sitting near the foot of the bed. I took a chair at its head. Two hours passed. Accustomed though she was to continued vigils, the attendant looked drowsy.

" I will watch," I motioned with my lips. " If I need help, I will wake you."

The woman gratefully assented and was soon breathing regularly and deeply. Another hour passed. Not for an instant did my eyes leave my father's face. Midnight came, and I saw, with the physician's trained vision, that a change had taken place. The sick man's countenance was no longer chalky gray, the lines around his mouth had relaxed, the forehead looked less parched. The crisis had come, had passed ; and my father would live !

Then, even as I softly rose, once again that brooding Horror filled the darkened room, and the abyss of my last sin yawned before me.

Why should I give the sick man the life that lay upon the table yonder? Hypodermic injections of the strychnia would stimulate the heart's feeble action to renewed life. The returning tide had only to be watched and fed to flow once again through the veins in the full measure of tranquil health. Meantime, what for me?

The wretched garret, the scanty food, the aimless wanderings through the squalid streets by night, the sinking yet deeper into the quicksand of evil practice. Stay my hand, no living man would be the wiser. " Heart failure " would be the unquestioned verdict over the death of the lamented Dr. Dudley.

Once again, as in a deadly nightmare, I knew the remorse that my act would bring in waking hours, but was without the power, nay, even the desire, to arouse myself. I revelled in the thought of the luxury that would again be mine. I scarcely breathed lest I should awake the nurse, whose nodding head caused me infinite amusement. I laid wagers with myself whether the death-rattle would arouse her; I smiled in joyful unison of thought and feeling to Something that was behind the screen, that was not there, nor here, nor anywhere, yet crushed upon my soul with all-pervasive force.

With eyes glued upon the face of my father, I noted with practised eyes each subtle symptom; saw life ebb away, and, ghoul-like, feasted upon the sight, and stirred neither hand nor foot.

The hours crept slowly on till that time when death comes oftenest. With the faint morning light my father opened his eyes in consciousness.

" George, my dear, dear boy ! " he murmured, made a motion as though to stretch out his arms to me, sighed faintly, and with that sigh breathed out his life — murdered, literally starved to death, by his son.

When It again left me, none of that list, whose first is Cain, suffered with my suffering.

As I had foreseen, my father had made no will, and I was sole heir. I am living in the house that was my home, but no servant remains with me four and twenty hours. No man calls me friend, and of them all none can answer why ! My sole resource is work, and far into the night I write the chapters on the " Pathology of the Mind " that will some day be given to the world that will no longer accept my daily labor.

I have prepared this record for the woman I have never ceased to love, to be given to her after my death. Perhaps what is dark in it may be clear to her higher light, her finer, purer spirit.

November 5. — Three weeks have elapsed since writing the above pages, and in all that time I have been *free*. Suppose — but I dare not picture to myself the possibility of a life free from curse. Yet since that tenth of September there has never been so long an interval that It has left me undisturbed.

November 6. — I saw and spoke with her
to-day, for the first time since that meeting in
my father's study. I dared not have spoken,
nor even have lifted my eyes to her face, but
she paused and held out her hand to me —
to *me!*

" Helena! " and as hands and eyes met, I
knew that her love was as changeless as my
own.

" I was sorry for your father's death," she
said. " I could not have grieved more, for
you and for myself, if I had really been the
daughter that I once thought to be," she
added, with her own directness and sim-
plicity.

" Sorry — for me? " I stammered.

" It has not been you I have blamed," she
made answer softly.

" May I come to see you — sometimes? "
I asked eagerly. " I — I would only remain
a few minutes. I would only look upon your
face, and go without a word," I pleaded.

Ah, the time when the evenings at her side
were all too short for both !

" It is better that you do not," she answered,
with more than the old-time gentleness. " My
prayers will always and forever be yours, but
— you have a wife," and to the sweet inex-
orableness of her tone I bared my head, for
to her the marriage service speaks with her

own truth, and what her God has joined together, only He can put asunder.

November 29. — Still free.

December 5. — Another week has passed
without Its presence. I have dared to picture
to myself the future, if It has left me for the
last time. Surely men would take me once
more by the hand when indefinable horror no
longer thrills them with the touch. Perhaps
Heaven, relentless to *my* prayers, may, in
answer to *hers*, vouchsafe me the mercy of
atonement, in small measure, for my sin, by
offering a life for a life. Yet, oh, if in that
future I could see one face, could have one
faint hope that on some blessed far-off day
Helena might be mine! — It is too much to
plead for happiness.

O God, if there be a God, I ask but the
opportunity of once again serving my fellow-
men!

Yet, come what may, I can never be alone
again, for I know that one heart is filled with
love for me. My darling, forgive me the
misery I have wrought you! I implore for
future as well as for past, for in spite of myself, my heart misgives me. Myself has
become a Horror.

December 10. — Two months have now
elapsed, and day by day hope grows brighter.
A servant has remained with me for a week.

I can see a change in my own face as I survey its features in the mirror, with the scrutiny of a girl of sixteen, on rising.

I dare to hope.

December 11. — For the first time for many months a patient has sought me. I could not have given him more flattering attention had I been a young physician with his first case. Moreover, the man himself interested me. He entered the office quietly, and described his symptoms with brevity and intelligence, unconsciously telling more than he uttered.

It appeared that he was a plumber by trade, and that while at work in a house at the old West End a rat had bitten him. He sought my advice regarding the unhealed wound.

"It seems that you are troubled with rats, too, sir," he remarked, as I examined his hand. "In fact, it is singular how many of the finest houses in the city are so infested. As soon as I step into a house, I see a rat scampering through the hall. Doesn't it disturb you when one races over the table like that?"

"Was there more than one?"

"There is never but one. He was like the fellow that bit me, with a long tail and red eyes. I have always been afraid of rats,—

I never undertake a job without tremor, —
although, as one may say, my life has been
passed amongst them. What! no fee?"

It would have been useless to argue with
my patient concerning his delusion. On
all other points perfectly sane, he doubtless
went about his business with as much intelligence as though he was not afflicted with
this curious mania. Arguments would have
been wasted in seeking to convince him of
the non-existence of the ghostly rat. He
might even have talked and compared notes
with a man having essentially the same
symptoms, and failed to recognize them as
his own. His case adds an interesting illus-
tration to the concluding chapter of my
"Pathology of the Mind."

December 12. — Glancing over the morning
newspaper, my eyes fell upon this item in the
list of "Deaths:"

"On the 11th inst., Mabel, wife of Fred-
erick Martin, aged twenty-three years, four
months."

My instant thought was Helena. I would
have asked no woman to share my shadowed
life, but now, when It has left me forever, and
the only bar, to her, to our union is removed,
she may be my wife. And perhaps, in time,
the memory of these darkened years — O
God! — again — Hel — Hel — e —

MARM PHŒBE'S FORTUNE

MARM PHŒBE sat erect in her favorite three-cornered chair in the parlor. A sontag, of some long-ago indeterminate color, was drawn tightly about her meagre shoulders. The mammoth white ruffles of a close-fitting cap, surmounted by a rampant bow of stiff black ribbon, framed a face that, brown as though stained with walnut juice, had the look of mingled fierceness and wistfulness not uncommon upon the faces of old women whose kinsfolk for generations have gone down to the sea in ships.

The wind had been " out " all day, and now, in the gloaming, its threat was fulfilled in the heavy drops of rain splashing against the many-paned windows. The room, with its low planchment, its hair-cloth furniture and wall-paper of stagnant green besprawled with livid spiders, had the musty smell peculiar to houses of great antiquity. Over the high, narrow mantel-shelf hung the portrait of the minister.

The woodeny features, the lack-lustre eyes and flaccid mouth of the canvas gave no hint of the personality that had played so momentous a part in the terrible drama that closed the seventeenth century in New England. There was a story, colored by the superstition rife amongst a seafaring folk, that pretended to explain why the artist, though of no mean repute in his day and generation, had so signally failed in what should have been the masterpiece of his art. In the possession of the minister was a negro slave woman named Tituba. She was of an unruly temper, and her master, after dealing with her with exemplary patience, sold her out of the country. Still, it may not have been an ill fate that consigned the old woman to the Portuguese trader, for in the terrible days of the witchcraft delusion, no one's life was safe from day to day, and a hasty word or a mere slip of the tongue, to say nothing of the ill-will of malicious folk, had sent even good and mild-mannered women to their death on Gallows Hill. But Tituba's rage at this unexpected disposition of what, in her froward temper, she had come to regard as her own body and soul knew no bounds, and her parting objurgation to her master was:

"Your pride shall go before your destruction."

The blow was well aimed, for pride might well have been called the besetting sin of the clergy, who aimed at nothing less than the supreme control of affairs, civil as well as ecclesiastical, in the new country. And was not the right divine of its authority receiving triumphant vindication in the undaunted front it presented in the present crisis — well depicted by the Reverend Cotton Mather as "that dark and diabolical confederation between Satan and some of the inhabitants, that threatened to overthrow and extirpate religion and morality, and to establish the kingdom of the Evil One in a country which had been dedicated by the prayers and tears and sufferings of its pious fathers to God and the Church."

Pride it was surely, too, although of a more personal and petty kind, that led the minister, who in sooth was a man of comely parts, to expend the sum realized from the sale of Tituba in having his portrait painted; but the result was disappointing, for strive as the artist would, only meaningless lines, flat surfaces, lifeless color, represented his reverend subject; but, meantime, in the background, there grew another face — one that the painter had never seen in life. Incessantly he overlaid his involuntary work with his darkest pigments. Out of the murky shadows the black face slowly emerged, and whether he would or no, the hapless artist must bestow upon its rendering the very triumph of his skill, till it stood upon the canvas instinct with life and wickedness and a wisdom not of this world.

For what work had he been hired? Did not the price of his labor represent Tituba, body and soul? Tooled by that insistent horror, he neither ate nor slept in the latter days of his task, and at its completion broke his brushes and went mad. In later days the tale was sometimes scoffed at. Small wonder, it was said, that the painter's hand had lost its cunning and hallucination clouded his brain, when he had "cried out" upon his own mother, and been witness to her death on Gallows Hill!

It was matter of history how, when the power of the clergy had reached its height, it was dealt its death-blow by Robert Calef, merchant, of Boston, in his book called the "History of the Witchcraft Delusion." Contumely fell upon the minister, as upon all those actively engaged in the persecution, and his last days were those of poverty and loneliness.

Let one seek to explain it as he would, there could be no doubt that the old slave woman's malediction had received repeated confirmation in every generation. Always had pride, the fulfilment of desire, been the precursor of destruction; ever, as the brimming cup touched the lip of the minister's ill-fated descendants, came the fatal slip!

In Revolutionary times there was the colonel, whose distinction it was to have steered the boat that conveyed Washington through the floating ice of the Delaware, to Trenton and victory. The Old Town welcomed its hero's return with frenzied patriotism; there were but few hours left of the night when the colonel, still clad in his buff and blue, cast himself into the three-cornered chair in his own parlor. There he was found in the murky morning light, huddled into an inert mass, his rigid fingers clutching his drawn sword, and a ghastly terror in the glazed, wide-open eyes fixed upon the portrait of the minister, or, as the gossips averred, upon a space a little above the minister's left shoulder. There was a sword-thrust through the canvas at that spot, which doubtless was the animus of the whispered tale of what it was that the dauntless soldier had vainly sought to master with carnal weapon. And there was none to suggest that the colonel may have drank once too often to the welfare of General Washington and the new government.

But if this evidence was not conclusive, what could be said of the fate of Marm

Phœbe's own father? Many times had the captain sailed out of the Old Town harbor, always to return in safety and with rich cargo, although those were the days when vessels were at the mercy of every contrary wind and delaying calm; when there must be braved the onslaught of Barbary pirates and the perils of the voyage around the Horn, before reaching the African coast and the East Indies, where new perils lay in wait in the greed and treachery of the natives. And now fresh danger menaced the Old Town merchantmen, in those depredations of the French war-craft that followed the war of 1812. That voyage of the brig " Cypher " to the coast of Africa was to be the last. The captain had embarked all his fortune in the venture, and the return freight of gold dust more than realized his fondest anticipations. But there was another reason besides the thought of the peaceful life he would henceforth lead on shore, in one of the stately mansions known as the " King's houses," for the captain's eagerness to sight the Old Fort. A child had been born to him in his absence — the child of his years. Her name — for with all a sailor's fervid piety, the captain felt no doubt that his prayer for " a little maid " would be answered — had been decided upon before his departure; and in the capacious blue sea-chest, covered with the intricate carvings of a sailor's jackknife, were wonderful playthings of coral and ivory, and a big carved work-box filled with marvellous trays, for the little girl who would soon be old enough to work her "sampler;" and in the captain's cabin hung a gilded cage with a green and gold parrot which had been taught to say "Phœbe," in whimsical anticipation of the tender word. It was the custom in the Old Town for the boys to lie in wait at the Old Fort when a vessel was expected home, and as soon as she came in sight to run with the joyful news to the sailors' wives; the expected gold dollar was always gladly paid. It was early one bright spring morning that the tidings of the brig "Cypher's" return were thus brought to little Phœbe's mother, who with her baby in her arms sped to the Old Fort. She was just in time to see the "Cypher" set upon by a French frigate that had been hovering about the coast for days, attracted by the rumor of the brig's rich freight. All the other ships of the Old Town, with its able-bodied men, were at sea; the frenzied remnant of the townsfolk gathered on the headland, and watched the fight, impotent.

Gallant defence was made, but what chance had the poorly armed merchantman against a fully equipped man-of-war? In one short hour the agonized wife saw the "Cypher" riddled with shot, boarded by the French, and the worthless hulk turned adrift.

Once, in her frenzy, when the fray was at its height, she held her baby high in her arms, out toward the scene of combat. A sailor, who, sorely wounded, was the only man on board the brig who succeeded in reaching the shore, told how, hard beset, the captain had suddenly seized his spyglass and directed it toward the Old Fort — an indiscretion for which he paid dearly, for the next moment the sword of the French captain was through his heart. A few days later, the wreck of the "Cypher" was cast upon the shore. Although the brig had been gutted of everything of intrinsic value, the ship's papers, the invoice of the cargo, and the captain's private diary were discovered intact, and, though drenched with sea water, still legible.

That was the story to which little Phœbe listened, almost at her mother's breast. "Tell it again!" and once more the child heard how her father had been cruelly murdered, and how the gold wrested from him was to be paid back to his wife and child. For, from the outset, it was expected that the American government would assume, as a tacit portion of the new treaty with France, the losses suffered by American shipping at the hands of its former allies. But delay and renewed promises and fresh complications repeated their weary round from year to year, and still the French Spoliation Claims were an unpaid debt to the descendants of the brave sea-captains of the early century.

But Phœbe never doubted.

"Will it be to-morrow?" and satisfied with the answer, the child went to sleep hugging to her heart the forlorn rag that was her childish "comfort."

"Coom, choild, don yur-rr c'losh, 'n' run fur-rr th' letter!" As far back as memory reached, that had been the twilight bidding.

In those far-off days the mail came by stage-coach, once a week, from Boston, and was deposited at the Fountain Inn. Phœbe must traverse the long, shingly stretch of beach that lay between, dodging misshapen bowlders, speeding past patches of quivering marsh-grass in which strange creatures lurked, and jumping pools of writhing seaweed, in whose slimy depths shapeless forms lay in wait; while the wind blew keenly from over the open sea, and the cries of the wraith of Barnegat, — the Shrieking Woman, — hideously murdered by Old Town pirates of eld, sounded in the child's ears, and gave the last touch of horror to the scene.

The French Spoliation Claims stood to little Phœbe for all the fairy-lore familiar to

more favored children. The three wishes of
elfin munificence, the possession of the purse
of Fortunatus, of Aladdin's lamp,— all of
richness and wonder would be realized when
the brig " Cypher's " freight was made good.
In that day she would play with golden grains
spread out like the sands of the seashore —
for in her fantasy it was the " Cypher's " gold-
dust that would be brought back intact; she
would have a monkey to play with, and a
green and gold parrot in a gilded cage, that
would say " Phœbe," like the one that was
told about in the last entry of her father's
diary.

As she grew older, if her dreams became
more restrained they were not less vivid. The
days of which her mother told — when the
Old Town had been the chief port of the East
India trade — should be restored in their
plenitude. Hogsheads of molasses, and rich,
spicy brown sugar should stand in the store-
room, with store of cocoanuts, and oranges,
and bananas, and tamarinds — out of which
to make delectable " tamarind water; " there
should be barrels of pickled limes; and of
guava jelly and other rich, strange, foreign
sweetmeats, galore. She would wear gowns
of cool seersucker and soft, lustrous India
silk, and would deck herself in rich cashmere
shawls and sweeping ostrich plumes; and she

would carry a sweet-smelling sandalwood fan and a carved ivory card-case.

Before Phœbe had fairly outgrown childhood, the burden of two lives was laid upon her shoulders. Her mother had never recovered from the shock of that hour at the Old Fort; incessant toil and meagre fare completed the ill work, and a stroke of paralysis rendered her helpless.

She sat, day after day, in the quaint old three-cornered chair, with her piercing eyes, to which had come the renewed vision sometimes bestowed by advanced years, never leaving the portrait over the mantel-shelf. Sometimes she would nod her head, and, pointing her skinny forefinger at the broken place in the canvas, utter shrill, unfathomable gibberish. Some hallucination concerned with the portrait she undoubtedly had, but it was not worth while to try to unravel the threadings of a tangled mind, nor, in a soil where every germ of superstition found rank growth, to heed the whisper that the old woman's marvellous vision had pierced beyond the shadows into the background of the picture.

At the best, Phœbe could earn but a meagre pittance oiling fishermen's clothes and " bushelling," as the rough mending of the fisherfolk was called; for the town had never recovered from the blow dealt its ship-

ping by the French war-craft, and its inter-
ests had dwindled to those of a mere fishing-
hamlet. Only once had a gleam of sunlight
found its way to Phœbe's darkened life. That
was when she and William Dolliver were
" keeping company." When or how the twain,
in their lives of incessant toil, found time to
make known their mutual love by so much
as a tender glance or a lingering pressure of
the hand could not be told; but one evening
Lum Dolliver asked Phœbe to accompany
him to the Old Fort, where time out of mind
Old Town lovers had strayed. It was then
that he put his arm around her and called her
his " sweetheart."

The next day, the fishing-smack of
which he was part owner set sail for the
Grand Banks, and was lost, with all on board,
in the well-remembered gale that swept away
most of the Old Town fishing-craft and
doomed the town to yet further narrowness
.and squalor. To Phœbe there came scarcely
a pang at her lover's loss. Youth and natural
desire had responded to that hour at the Old
Fort, but one idea had dominated her life too
long to be easily supplanted by another.

The Old Town had always held itself aloof
from its neighbors, in a certain inexplicable
pride of isolation. Following the September
gale, no breath of the world's great life ever

reached its borders; widowed and orphaned,
its women, with strange, fierce resentment
against a world that had no sorrow like unto
their sorrow, hooted the stranger from out
the ways; the very children stoned the vent-
uresome traveller who set foot within its con-
fines. Even the houses seemed to have
caught the infection of sullen hermithood,
and with their bull's-eye doors and the queer
outside staircases known as "standards,"
climbed up on the high rocky ledges, drew
up their skirts around them, and sat down
with their backs upon the labyrinth of narrow, crooked lanes below.

One morning Marm Phœbe's mother was
found dead in the three-cornered chair, her
wide-open eyes still fixed upon the minister's
portrait. An old woman, if not in years, in
stiffened limbs and stiffer habits of life, Marm
Phœbe lived on alone — with the added misery of not knowing her own loneliness. The
visions of comfort and plenty had disap-
peared like the fantasies of her childhood.
Merely to touch and handle the gold, to dab-
ble her hands in the yellow grains and let
them slip through her fingers, — in that
thought she lived and moved and had her
being. It mattered not that to the generation
that had arisen "Marm Phœbe's fortune" was
a legend, classed with that of the Shrieking

Woman. Every twilight the quaint green calash appeared at the window of the post-office with the query, " Has th' letter coom?" and at the inevitable answer turned away — to wait till to-morrow. Hope was not the lovely being hidden in the box of Troubles. It was the terrible Old Man of the Sea, strangled in one form only to reappear in another hideous, mocking shape.

She had not failed to-night of her usual mission because of a first faint chill mis-giving; at least, none was present to her active consciousness. She had the molly-grubs, she told herself, and her customary supper of dry bread, and tea without milk or sugar, had not " set jist right."

There was a tap at the window. The stunted figure of the postmaster's son stood on tiptoe without, wildly waving some white object. Marm Phœbe raised the window a crack.

" Chuck!" called out the boy, and a letter whirled across the room. The messen-ger was off like the wind, and Marm Phœbe shut the window, secured its primitive fasten-ing, closed the inside shutters, and deliberately hooked the upper and lower set. Then she lit the lamp and picked up the big envelope. There was no thrill of happy surmise in the touch, deliciously prolonged by toying with the missive, by examining the official imprint in the corner, by playing at ignorance of its contents. The world held but one letter. The expected had happened.

She searched in her work-basket for the scissors, cut open the envelope, and read, word by word, the formal statement of the Court of Claims: in effect, that the evidence respecting the brig " Cypher " had been admitted, and reimbursement made accordingly, out of the French Spoliation Fund. Accompanying was another paper.

It was a treasury warrant for one hundred and fifty thousand dollars.

Hope sloughed once again, and snaked forth — Realization; and its substance was shadow, and its grasp nothingness.

A wave of loneliness and emptiness and unutterable desolation swept over Marm Phœbe. The very reason and substance of being had been stricken from her, and all she had in its stead was a scrap of paper! And her head ached, and her eyes swam, and she was strangely tired. From some undefined impulse that perhaps had its root in an unrecognized need of sympathy, perhaps from an undefined distrust of the shadows on the portrait, she glanced suddenly upward, but only the woodeny features of her reverend ancestor responded.

She was conscious of a vague discomfort, as though some one, invisible to her, was watching her intently; there was a reflection of her mother's demented rage in the resentment that glowed dully against somebody who was spying upon her. Wait, she would fix the old witch-woman! She would turn her portrait face to the wall!

With frenzied haste Marm Phœbe dragged the chair to the mantel-shelf, mounted it, and, exerting all her strength, swung the portrait around. The extent of the injury done by the colonel in his drunken rage was thus revealed; the sword had broken through the thin board backing, and as the picture was removed from its support against the wall, a splinter fell away, revealing a roll of parchment that had been carefully concealed in the interior. Marm Phœbe pulled it out, without surprise or curiosity. In the strange numbness that seemed to be stealing over her mental faculties as well as her physical members, if the minister himself had stepped out and down from the frame, it would scarcely have aroused emotion. She drew near the lamp and prepared to read the message so strangely brought to light, in the perfunctory way in which one might peruse an indifferent letter placed in one's hand. She recognized the quaint, crabbed hand-

writing of the parchment as the minister's;
and even to her beclouded faculties straggled
the perception that her reverend ancestor
had taken advantage of the ill repute of his
own portrait to consign some secret to its
keeping.

I write these Pages — y⁰ Inner Recᵈ of y⁰ Proceed-
ings that have, of late, inflamᵈ All New England —
that future Generations may justify Mine Own Conduct
therein, & that of y⁰ Holy Man of God, y⁰ Revᵈ Cotton Mather.

My Daughter Elizabeth & My Niece Abigail found
Plesure in listening to y⁰ Tales of my old Negro Slave
Woman, Tituba by Name, bought by mee whilst a
Merchant in y⁰ Spanish Main. More especially they
hearkened to her Narrative of a Strange Powʳ pos-
sessᵈ by some of her Race, known as Hoodoo, & by
them chiefly used to y⁰ Discomfiture of their Enemies.
For a long Time, y⁰ Old Woman professed to bee un-
able, herself, to Produce any of These same Marvells;
but y⁰ fervid Intrest of y⁰ Children at last moved her
to give some slight Attestation of y⁰ Strange Powʳ.
Y⁰ Story was privily Whispered to a Playmate, Ann
Putnam by Name & Tituba Yieldᵈ, after no Great
Solicitation, to y⁰ Pleading, " Do it again." By Hints
& Mysterious half told Tales, y⁰ Curiosity of various
Goodwives in y⁰ Neighborhood was now aroused & y⁰
Circle gradually Increasᵈ, meeting Regularly at y⁰
Houses of y⁰ Different Members, at such Times as
y⁰ Goodman of y⁰ House might bee absent. One
after Another of y⁰ Circle, intoxicated by y⁰ Discovery
of her own Possession of y⁰ Strange Powʳ, was led
Farther & yet Farther, to its Excise. I will add that
Goodwife Bishop, Goodwife Corey & Others who suf-

fered Death as Witches upon Gallows Hill, began their Practises with no Other Intent than y⁰ Gratification of Their Idle Curiosity; misled by y⁰ Strange Powʳ so unexpectedly evoked, they put it to Unlawful Ends, & Whither it may carry any one not having y⁰ Fear of God before his Eyes, I know not.

Of All y⁰ Arts known to Tituba, I am not acquainted; but Chief amongst Them, when she would Practise upon One Present in y⁰ Flesh, was to hold Before his Eyes a Certain Bright Stone, — always worn by her around her Neck, — with y⁰ Result, too Marvellous of Credence had I not been Privily Witness thereto, of Producing a Belief in All Manner of Unrealities; & what may bee y⁰ Limits of y⁰ Strange Powʳ, in Extent, or Time, or Space, is not for mee to Affirm. But thus far it is given mee to Speak with Certitude.

There bee a Certain Powʳ invested in Men, by wᶜʰ, with y⁰ Aid of a Bright Stone or like Object, held close before y⁰ Eyes, they may exert Strange Influence over their Fellow Beings, so that these last shall have no Sense, nor Desire, nor Will, save that of their Masters. They shall shrink from no Command that is laid upon them; they shall Think & Talk & Act, like Creatures Possessᵈ of Understanding, yet be without Present Wit or after Recollection, of that wᶜʰ they have thought & said & wrought; & y⁰ Knowledge of y⁰ Strange Powʳ was possessᵈ by Prophets & Wise Men of old, in y⁰ far East & in y⁰ Land of y⁰ Pharaohs; & it was Guarded by these from y⁰ People, to y⁰ Great Furthrance of y⁰ Might of y⁰ Priesthood. & This it is given to mee to Speak upon y⁰ Attestation of y⁰ Revᵈ Cotton Mather, who in his great Learning & his Knowledge of many Tongues, had Acquaintance with y⁰ Strange Powʳ. Of y⁰ Extent of his Knowledge & whether he himself practised therein, I know naught, & This I do affirm upon my most Solemn Oath.

His Acquaintance with yᵉ Events here set down followed close upon Mine Own, for I deemed it wise to obtain yᵉ Light of his great Learning & Piety upon Matters wᶜʰ pressed heavily upon mine Own Humble Understanding. It was my farther good Hap, to receive from him, from Time to Time, divers & various Instructions how to fan yᵉ Spark into a Blaze, for yᵉ Maintenance & greater Powʳ of yᵉ Church in New England, whose Champion he was, So that, to use the words of his own Pious Exhortation, " It shall enable us so to Box it about amongst ourselves, till it come I know not where, at last."

Let them who raise yᵉ Spell, beware yᵉ Fiend. Yᵉ Madness of yᵉ People went beyond Guidance or Control; & as it was written, " Yᵉ Brother shall betray yᵉ Brother to Deathe & yᵉ Fathʳ yᵉ Son; & Children shall rise up against their Parents & shall cause Them to bee put to Deathe," aye, even to yᵉ Heavy Deathe.

Yᵉ Humor of yᵉ People veered & catching up yᵉ Bell of yᵉ Arch Traitor & Infidel, Robᵗ Calef, Merchant, of Boston, hound upon us with yᵉ Cry, " Delusion! " Yᵉ Revᵈ Cotton Mather is reviled & insulted in yᵉ very Streets of Boston, late yᵉ Citadel of God's Powʳ in yᵉ New World. Yᵉ Judge who passed Sentence upon those now termed " Martyrs " doeth, yearly, Public Penance for his Unjust Judgments. I am cried out Upon for greater Wickedness than any proven against those who sufferᵈ. Yᵉ Civic Powʳ of yᵉ Clergy is , stricken from them forever; nay, its Powʳ in yᵉ Spiritual Guidance of yᵉ People has recᵈ so deadly a Blow that henceforth & forever, we shall bee looked upon but as Blind Mouths. Blood will swim before Men's Eyes when they turn them upon God's Ministers, and good Men & True shall Turn themselves away from Ghostly Counsel.

Y^e Witches were no "Martyrs." They met their just Deserts.

When, Centuries hence, Men shall have recov^d from ye Evil Days upon wch we are fallen & shall seek Enlightened Understanding of ye Strange Pow^r, not to ye Flickring Strength of Priestcraft shall Knowledge bee given.

Unto that day, committing ye Discovery of these Pages to ye Providence Men call Chance, I leave my Words of Revelation & Warning.

"Cat's foot!" ejaculated Marm Phœbe. Witchcraft, as embodied in the old tales of a midnight mass presided over by a black man with a long, narrow red book, — the ledger of lost souls, — might have ground for belief; uncanny concomitant stories familiar in the Old Town bore out its plausibility. There was Lum Dolliver's mother, who saw the vessel that bore her son to destruction take on the form of a shroud as it rounded the Old Fort. And had not Marm Cas'll, at the very moment her twin brother was drowned off the Horn, awaked with the taste of salt water in her mouth, and the sensation of being strangled? But this stuff about a "strange power" that made people puppets in its hands was not to be hearkened to by any one who knew how many blue beans it took to make seven.

Without more ado, Marm Phœbe held the MS., sheet by sheet, over the flame of the lamp, and watched them consume to her finger tips. As though the blaze of that last scrap of paper possessed, like the dervish's ointment, some mystic power of illumination, for the space of its brief light there glowed before her mental vision the utmost meaning and glory of her wealth. The golden fantasies of childhood, the dreams of peace and plenty of her maturer years, the rapture of handling the vast sum over which her age had gloated, — all, all were hers! The salt breath of the ocean fanned her cheek; she felt the touch of Lum Dolliver's strong, manly arm, and heard his whisper, " My sweetheart!"

Not from her parched lip had the brimming cup been dashed!

Wait, she would show the fortune to the black woman who was always trying to wreak her vengeance upon her and hers. She would flaunt the priceless paper in Tituba's face and scoff her and laugh at her! With frenzied haste Marm Phœbe pushed the chair to the mantel-shelf again, and replaced the minister's portrait in its position. Somewhere, out there in the shadows, Tituba was lurking. She could see, if she could not be seen. She should part her huge lips and gnash her hideous white teeth, impotent!

Marm Phœbe turned to the table. The scrap of paper was not there. She searched the floor, the chairs, and even peered behind the shutters, in vain. Bewildered, her unthinking glance rested on the heap of charred fragments beside the lamp, and the truth burst upon her.

She had burnt the treasury warrant!

The face of the minister had become blurred. What gleamed there over his shoulder — a double gleam, like the white of glaring eyeballs! The background of the picture was melting away. What was that coming nearer — and yet nearer! Why should mere shadows take on a look of unspeakable, monstrous triumph!

"She was took like her mother," said the neighbors the following day, when Marm Phœbe was found huddled into an inert heap on the parlor floor. One rigid hand clutched a round of the three-cornered chair, and the lack-lustre eyes were fixed, in their last gaze, upon the portrait of the minister.

THE students had gathered around the figure that the master was displaying. The distorted features, the strained muscles, the agonized tension of the fingers, were exquisitely wrought in a composition of tawny red, shading into bronze. After a brief glance, a short, thick-set girl, with coarse, black hair and a freckled face, returned to her work.

"It is a miniature copy of the life-size original in the museum at Montevideo," explained the master. "There had been a battle between the Spaniards and the Indians. Whichever side wins in these frequent outbreaks, the half-breeds — the Gauchos—suffer. If one asks, 'Were many killed?' the reply is, 'Oh, only a few Gauchos,' as though they were vermin. I went to the battlefield after the fight. This fellow lay gasping for water. Luckily, the brook was at some distance, and I worked fast. Look at the pose!" he added, with enthusiasm. He spoke as he had acted when a dying man's unslaked agony was the price of his art.

Margaret Lane returned to her place at last beside the girl with the coarse face and coarser ways.

" How could you look upon the man's suffering? " demanded the latter, and her voice completed the impression of a hard, assertive personality.

" Art is impersonal," answered the other girl coldly, in her clear, full-toned enunciation.

" The artist cannot separate himself from his art," said Martha Graves, vehemently; " no one can rise above his own level."

" Have you been long in a position to define art? " inquired Miss Lane, courteously.

Usually she sought no reason for her instant attractions and antipathies, perhaps even priding herself upon them as part and proof of the artistic temperament. But her dislike of Martha Graves — dating from her first glance at the latter's work — she had sedulously sought to justify. And ample cause surely lay in her neighbor's shabby, often untidy gown, her thick, repulsive fingers, more suited to factory work than to the delicate manipulation of clay; deeper still in the fact that she had been working in a Brockton shoe-shop; and that a common mill-hand should presume to enter a sculptor's studio was an insult to art to be justly resented by one who had been born and bred in the inner circles of Boston culture.

Perhaps it was because Margaret Lane's example was infectious that Martha Graves' easel, the solitary exception, was never surrounded by a group of fellow-students, and assailed by the free, bold criticism that is in itself so important an element of class work. Not so much as a passing glance was ever vouchsafed the efforts, presumptuous if not so ludicrous, of the factory girl. But her coarse-fibred, positive nature was proof against the silent snubs and unspoken dislike, even if she noticed them; she only worked with feverish energy, and was the first to come and the last to leave the studio.

No one knew how it had leaked out that Martha Graves' art education was a hand to mouth struggle, and that her sole means of support were the savings from her meagre wages in the shoe factory. Her sack was threadbare, and her overshoes but a mockery of protection against the snow and slush of an unusually severe winter. She lived in a hall bedroom, three flights back, in a narrow, sunless street in a squalid part of the South End, where she prepared her own scanty meals over a little ill-smelling kerosene stove. There was a seamstress who had a room on the same floor, who was occasionally employed by Mrs. Lane. Margaret Lane held herself above listening to "servants' tattle," but a few chance words concerning the seamstress's neighbor may have fallen on her unheeding ears. There was no one to guess that Martha Graves' present life was the bright and beautiful realization of the dream of a lifetime.

For the past few weeks the atmosphere of the studio had been rarefied with struggle. A well-known art-patron had offered a scholarship — three years' study abroad — to the pupil who should produce the best piece of work within a specified time. Margaret Lane's choice of subject was the thorn-crowned head of Christ. Martha Graves' was a satyr's head. Both girls were working from photographs. The present week closed the time allowed for the work, when the various clay models were to be cast in plaster and submitted to the art committee.

In cold, impartial self-criticism, Margaret Lane had measured her own work against that of the others, and knew that there could be no doubt of the issue. In another week her name would be on every one's lips as the winner of the most important art scholarship

of the year, and she drew a long breath of
rapture as the future arose before her.   Three
years in Italy, consecrated to art, and with
the inspiring consciousness that her own
talent had paved the way! A scornful look
crossed her face as she thought of Martha
Graves and her delusion. Almost, at that
moment of exaltation, she could have pitied
her!
    Her neighbor had not been in the studio
to-day nor yesterday. Some impulse of auto-
matic memory recalled the fact that Martha
Graves had been absent since the morning
they had exchanged impressions regarding the
Dying Gaucho. Led by a sudden impulse
that was perhaps mere aimless curiosity,
perhaps an undefined misgiving that was
strangely tangled with her " antipathy,"
Margaret Lane withdrew the wrappings from
Martha Graves' work and stood transfixed.
    Into the clay had been instilled the love
of mischief, allied to moral irresponsibility,
the working of evil ends without evil intent
or stain of sin, whose possibility had ceased
with the evolution of the higher life. It was
the satyr of heathen art, and not since the
days of heathen art had such a conception
found form!
    A few more touches, scarcely lacking even
to critical eyes, and then for Martha Graves

the years in the atmosphere that would be the breath of home to her exiled soul, and which would unfold in her that which Margaret Lane knew her own utmost striving could never attain.

In order to keep the clay moist and plastic, at the close of the day's work it was wet down, either by lightly sprinkling with the hand or by spraying with an atomizer, and covered with cotton and rubber swathings. During Martha Graves' absence no friendly hand had cared for her work, and the clay was already hard and dry.

With practised eyes Margaret Lane saw that if the satyr's head was not wet without delay, another twenty-four hours would see it ruined. All at once she recalled something that the seamstress had said about Miss Graves having a cold; "threatened with pneumonia" — were not those the words?

Dizzy with a sudden emotion that she could not, or would not, analyze, Margaret Lane leaned heavily against the easel. Out of the black mist came a flash that wellnigh blinded and stunned her. It was generated by the fusion of two thoughts.

Martha Graves could not leave her bed. Twenty-four hours closed the contest.

With her hand clutching the atomizer, she lived years in the next few seconds. For a

friend's sake, her haughty, self-sufficient
rectitude might have overcome. But how
could she sacrifice her own future for the sake
of the hated factory girl! Only a moment
ago she had been cheated into a thought of
pity for Martha Graves' fatuity — and her
face burned at her own vast presumption!
The master was approaching. No other eye
must look upon this work. With tender,
loving reverence, she replaced the swathings
of the satyr's head.

The following day, as the light was waning,
the studio door was pushed rudely open and
a shabbily dressed girl entered, breathing
heavily and holding one hand to her chest.
Without noticing any one, Martha Graves
walked to her easel and withdrew carefully,
but in evident distracted haste, the coverings
from the clay. The girl by her side heard
the hoarse panting and knew that it was
not caused by "threatened pneumonia." A
student on the other side of the room was
" packing the board; " that is, taking hand-
fuls of damp clay from the chest and flinging
them at his feet, into a mass that was to be
wrought into high relief. Margaret Lane
counted the thuds as though their enumera-
tion was her chief concern in life.

" It is finished ! " sounded the coarse voice.
What fantasy was it that the utterance

brought to mind the words, spoken long ago, by one who hung upon the cross? Margaret Lane nerved herself to glance at her neighbor's work.

The clay was dry and shrunken, and a fine network of lines, like the "crackle" of porcelain, had taken the youth from the face, while its expression of chaste and buoyant sensuousness was curiously transformed to that of bestial cunning by a jagged fissure, leering from one eye to a corner of the mouth. Envy, hatred, malice, and all uncharitableness mocked from the altered features, in the distorted strength that has made deliberate choice of evil. Irresponsibility was gone; the creature of the woods and fields was replaced by man, after the revelation of his higher nature, and with its claims ruthlessly trampled upon.

"Your work is quite spoiled. What a pity!" said Miss Lane, with conventional smoothness, and despised herself for the petty hypocrisy. She worked steadily on. Blind and dizzy with exultation, her very being seemed to impart itself to those last light touches on the impressionable clay.

Thud, thud!

"It sounds like the first handful of earth upon the coffin," said the strident voice of the factory hand. "You've never heard it" —

with a glance at her own black gown — " or
maybe you'd be different. The doctor said I
mustn't leave the bed, but I'd have come if
I'd crawled on my hands and knees. I've
read how, in ancient Egypt, when a mother
killed her child, the lifeless body was strapped
to her. I don't wonder that those women went
mad."

With a kind of passionate tenderness, she
wrapped the coverings about her work; and
thrusting it under her arm, went out into the
cold and dark.

When the result of the competition was
made known, to every one's surprise the
scholarship was awarded, not to the favorite
student, but to a young man of whom no one
had thought in that connection.

.   .   .   .

It was the day of the crowning triumph of
Margaret Lane's life. The statue that she
had moulded in the clay which is the life, had
looked upon in the plaster which is the
death, was to be unveiled to-day in the
marble which is the resurrection.

The throng of people, distinguished visitors, famous artists and dignitaries of Church
and State, had come together to do honor —
not to her, — that thought held no share in
the sweet, glad consciousness of acknowl-

edged power, — but to her work. Speeches had been made, poems read, and now loud huzzas sounded as the statue gleamed in the sunlight and a tall, calm-faced woman arose from her place at the governor's side.

The twenty years that had passed had brought to Margaret Lane the crowning glory of a strong and beautiful womanhood. When or how the Voice had spoken to her does not matter. Enough that she had listened, and her consecrated life witnessed the reality of the new birth.

Love and sympathy, the priceless flowers of the spiritual qualities that her hard, brilliant girlhood had lacked, were fused into intellectual insight and the results of a masterly technique; men spoke of her "genius;" but, impartial as ever in her self-appraisal, Margaret Lane knew that hers was but the five-fold talent. Genius she had never seen but once.

There was a door of her past life that her present self never opened. In her studio was a box containing a plaster cast sent back in curt dismissal twenty years ago.

As she reseated herself in the carriage, a woman, who, despite the commands and buffetings of the police, had thrust and elbowed her way through the surging crowd, stood almost under the carriage wheels, and the governor, leaning forward, spoke a kindly word of warning. It was a woman with a hard, mean face, whose features, set as though in some strange arrested development, seemed to offer no chance of appeal to a finer and truer nature that some congenial atmosphere might once have developed. A fetid odor arose from her untidy clothes, as from long contact with rank leather. For a second the eyes of the two women met, and before those of Margaret Lane was unveiled the slow, hideous process of a soul's dissolution.

She had returned to her studio. Perhaps she was impelled by some impulse she would not question, perhaps it was her whim to see from the critical height of to-day, the work that represented the joyous anticipation and bitter disappointment of her youth. With haste strangely at variance with her usual calm demeanor, she drew the nails from the box containing the plaster cast, and looked upon that which her hands had wrought twenty years ago.

Had it been that the impression made by Martha Graves' wonderful art upon a keenly susceptible nature had influenced her own work to the extent of unconscious imitation? Was it that she had looked upon a monstrosity in that mystic moment of supreme sensitiveness, when her own conception was still in the womb, and it had come forth stamped with a hideous birthmark? Or did this abortion embody a truth deeper still, more inscrutable?

Dimly, yet overpoweringly, the revelation sank into her soul.

Upon the Christ nature within herself had her hand been raised. Her sin looked at her from the very face of Him who had become her Master. For instead of the inner life that had illumined and glorified the physical beauty and commanding intellect, were stamped envy, hatred, malice, and all un-charitableness.

From the face of the Christ, the satyr mocked and leered.

THE PORTRAIT BY HUNT

IT was the last day of the Loan Exhibition, held in the "sloyd" room of the Industrial School. If the thinly clad, apathetic throng, of varied nationality, may have lingered longer over circus posters and the flaring announcements of the latest theatrical sensation than before the gigantic Bierstadt, the moonlight of De Haas, the sunset of Turner, or even the "Burial of a Mummy," which, depicted in all the richness and stateliness of a far-off age, yet seemed to strike a common chord of humanity, their lack of appreciation was merely proof of the timeliness of the present exhibition. "To raise the masses" being the popular cry, it was desirable to begin at the right end, and be sure that they learnt, betimes, to distinguish between a Bouguereau and a Bridgman, with which worthy intent, two ladies, members of the committee, whose list comprised many well-known names, had been in daily attendance.

It was drawing near the hour for closing, and the only visitor now was the old woman employed to do the scrubbing about the building, drawn thither, perhaps, less from love of art than desire for warmth, for the drizzling rain had changed to a driving storm of alternate snow and sleet.

Old Betty was a familiar figure to visitors at the school as she tugged her heavy pail of water over the stairs or wrung out mopping-rags with hands gnarled and distorted with rheumatism and ceaseless toil, and chapped and cracked with suds and exposure. The tattered, dingy fragment of a shawl was tied about her head, the fringe of which mingled with the elf-locks of coarse, gray hair that streamed about her wrinkled, haggard face. Her calico skirts, pinned up over a short patched petticoat, of long ago indeterminate color, revealed the clumsy stockings and heavy boots, which made additional misery for the swollen feet.

Mrs. De Long, beautiful in her serene, gracious matronhood, explained the pictures, one by one, till they reached the gem of the collection, in its magnificent frame of Venetian scroll-work, before which the most indifferent spectator had lingered.

It was the portrait of a young girl, with shining masses of brown hair drawn to a loose knot at the back of her head, and frank, sunny eyes with a smile in their brown depths that matched the curves of the lovely mouth. It was a happy, fearless face, with the look of one who feels that for her the world holds all good things. Her gown, a pale pink brocade, was thrown into relief by dark crimson draperies; one slender, white hand drooped with the weight of a feather fan.

The broad treatment, the delicate, harmonious coloring, the tender, poetic feeling, so rich, yet restrained in suggestiveness, gave it rank as the artist's best work.

Mrs. De Long would have passed with the murmured words, " A portrait by Hunt," but old Betty, wearied with her long day's work, had sunk upon a chair near by.

" Stay and rest," said Mrs. De Long, laying a gentle, kindly hand upon the old woman's shoulder, as she lingered for a moment before the picture, suddenly thrown into strong relief by the electric light over the corner grocery opposite. Then returning to her friend, in the low-voiced talk that followed, the old woman's presence was forgotten.

" You cannot think how startled I was to see that picture there," began Mrs. De Long.

" It is of some one whom you know?" queried Mrs. Morris.

" It is the portrait of Elizabeth Gair," was the reply.

" I wonder that others have not recognized it," resumed Mrs. De Long after a lengthened silence, which her friend instinctively forbore to break. "But all the Gairs are dead; family friends, too, are dead or scattered, and perhaps if any one did recognize the picture, he deemed silence best. Elizabeth Gair was the most beautiful creature I ever saw. The portrait does not do her justice — no art could. It hung over the mantel-shelf in the Gair drawing-room; and then, as now, seemed to absorb all the light in the room. I have seen many a visitor pause on the threshold, forgetful even of greeting, spell-bound by the vision before him. Poor Elizabeth Gair ! " and the womanly voice faltered.

"I was much in the Gair house. Elizabeth's sister Nellie was my most intimate friend. We looked up to Elizabeth with the enthusiasm of young girls for one a few years their senior, who represents to them all that is admirable in womanhood. Her party gowns, her dainty shoes, the exquisite stockings of finest silk, the gloves that looked almost too small even for hands that had nothing to do but carry flowers or toy with a fan — were the objects of our wondering adoration. We loved to touch, with reverent finger-tips, the dainty shimmering things, as they lay outspread upon the bed, in readiness for the evening's festivity. She was so good to us! We would sit at her feet for hours, listening to stories of the gay world in which she bore her part so admirably. That bright anticipation of the pictured face is only a feeble representation of what beamed from hers. Her beauty was the smallest part of her charm. That lay in the graciousness, the lovableness of her personality; in its power of drawing out the best that there was in every one, no matter how deeply, how apparently hopelessly, it lay buried. Never have I known a nature in which the rare magnetism of goodness was so potent as in Elizabeth Gair's.

" I can scarcely speak of the end, even at the distance of nearly thirty years. There came a time when her name was on every one's lips. But not — not as it had been spoken.

" No gossip could even surmise how it happened. · To have married Elizabeth Gair would have seemed the realization of the proudest dream of any man.

" Her picture was taken from the wall. I supposed, till to-day, that it was destroyed. Her father forbade her name to be mentioned in his presence. Nellie, nearly heart-broken, was sent away to school. Contrary to all the conflicting stories, Elizabeth did not leave her father's house. A room was fitted up for her in the upper story, where, with locked doors and shut and shuttered windows, — the only glimpse of the sky a narrow rift at the top, — Elizabeth Gair lived for five long years, without speech with any one, allowed only her books and embroidery for companionship.

"Nellie passed her vacations either at school or with an aunt whose home was in a distant city. It was during one of these visits that her engagement took place. An early marriage was advisable, for the girl was practically without a home. Family pride, however, dictated that the marriage should take place from her father's house.

" Nellie's tears and pleadings to see her sister again — for the last time — finally prevailed. Just before the bridal party set out for the church, Elizabeth was conducted to the drawing-room. Did the sight of the beautiful apartment, whose chief ornament had once hung in that blank space over the mantel-shelf; the meeting with the little sister, grown to womanhood in the five years' blank of her own existence; the thought that she had forfeited the right to stand by Nellie's side, the loving, beloved elder sister, in this, the supreme hour of the girl's life, — did it all bring home to Elizabeth, as never before, what had been — and what was?

" Nellie never told me what passed between them at that interview.

" Soon after the wedding, the announcement of Elizabeth Gair's death appeared in the daily papers. It may have been true. Ah, how often I have prayed that it was true! The house was closed and Mr. and Mrs. Gair went abroad; within a year both were dead. Nellie's death had preceded theirs; the property went to a distant cousin and the household furnishings were scattered far and wide.

" I don't like to speak of what I heard. Probably there was not a word of truth in it. Elizabeth Gair was dead. But in one of those curious, roundabout ways in which tidings that affect us most deeply reach us in indifferent speech, I heard mention of a ball given annually by a notorious woman for the leaders of the demi-monde, and frequented by the best men — so called — in town. On one of these occasions, the gayest of the gay, a woman with the light of utter recklessness in her beautiful eyes, outdoing all the others in her abandonment of every good and womanly impulse, was she who had once been — I cannot speak the name in such connection, even now. Never do I see a painted creature but that my heart beats high. Anywhere, anyhow, I should know her; no matter how changed by time or circumstances, a voice would whisper, ' It is she,' and I should hear its accents, however low and indistinct.

"Never were there gifts so utterly wasted; never was there a life so wrecked beyond redemption as Elizabeth Gair's!

" I don't know why I have told you the story," added Mrs. De Long, hurriedly. " It is the first time it has crossed my lips. But I felt impelled to speak. Perhaps it was the influence of the twilight, the storm, or the unexpected sight of that picture, that has made me feel so uneasy, so distraught."

Whatever the undercurrent of their thoughts, when the two ladies spoke again it was upon indifferent subjects; of the Exhibition, of matters of social interest, and, presently, of church topics, — " chapters " and "missions" and " board meetings." The old woman, lulled perhaps by the gentle murmur of their voices and by the grateful warmth of the room, with head bowed upon the " sloyd " bench before her, had apparently fallen asleep.

A name was mentioned — that of the rector.

" They say he will leave us, if he receives the call," said Mrs. De Long. " Besides be-

ing the most influential church in the diocese,
it is the open road to the bishopric."

"Personal ambition could not influence
Mr. Bache," responded Mrs. Morris, with
gentle reproach. "But if he should accept,
what a loss he would be to us! How we
should miss that ineffable smile, the pressure
of the beautiful white hands, that look out of
the soulful eyes that says so much without
utterance!"

"Rev. Francis Bache is wise in confining
his intercourse with the feminine contingent
of his pastoral charge to that dumb eloquence
which, like Goethe's definition of a Märchen,
may mean everything, or nothing," answered
Mrs. De Long, dryly.

"My dear," expostulated Mrs. Morris, "I
am sure you admire and reverence our rector
as much as any one — are as deeply in spiritual sympathy with his exalted ideals. You
keep Lent most rigorously, go to all the early
services, and never miss attendance on Sun-
days and feast days."

"I go to his church," responded Mrs. De
Long, in clear, hard tones, "because his sermons are pleasing to the intellect. I enjoy
his vivid word-pictures and the faculty he
has of seeming to single me out from all
the congregation ; and because, toward that
peculiar union of the æsthetic and the emo-

tional in which lies his greatest power, I con-
fess to being in the mental attitude of the
small boy convicted over a dime novel: ' I
like to have my blood curdled ! ' But when,"
continued Mrs. De Long, in another tone,
" in those moments of soul-hunger that come
to us all, I have cried out for bread, he has
given me but a stone. What do I care that
it is a beautiful, glittering stone, that the
world calls a gem ! "

" You have known him a long while?"
queried Mrs. Morris, with interest.

" I knew him before he entered the pulpit;
' Francis Bache turn minister ! ' was the exclamation. That the gay young fellow, the
leader in every social frolic, should renounce
the world was as sudden and miraculous a
conversion as St. Paul's. I thought so, too,
then. I have changed my opinion since.
Ambition was the key-note of Francis Bache's
character then, as now. The personal magnetism that drew towards him so irresistibly
maid and matron, the charm with which he
invested the lightest word, making you feel
that it was addressed to you alone, — although
not precisely as a miserable sinner, — the
exquisite modulation of tone that made him
the most admirable Claude Melnotte the
amateur stage has ever seen, were held even
then as the tools with which, presently, he

would build the ladder to eminence. Meanwhile, that union of the emotional and æsthetic, which with him took the place of a
coarser passion, should have its fling, never
forgetting that one false step would ruin the
whole lofty scheme. Why has he never
married? is often asked. Because of personal aggrandizement. Only a celibate priest
may attain eminence. Even in appearance
he is unchanged. The slight, graceful figure,
the smooth face, the burning dark eyes,
are the same now that they were thirty years
ago."

The janitor knocked at the door presently.
It was the hour for closing the building. The
ladies' carriage was waiting. "The old
woman is still there," hesitated Mrs. Morris.

"Let the poor creature remain; she can
do no harm," returned Mrs. De Long, shivering as she drew her furred wraps about her.
"She is familiar with the building, and the
janitor's door will be unlocked."

The room was left to the darkness — save
where the electric light focused its dazzling
radiance — and to the old woman.

She raised her head at last, and gazed at
the portrait with an agony that could not
find expression in tears; eyes such as hers
lose their power of weeping. Her hands
were outstretched, as in pity and supplication.

"I've heard your story, dear," she whispered, "and every word fell on my heart. There was no one in all the world to hold out a hand to you, not even when you went to the window and looked up at the stars shining in the chink of sky they had left you, and cried in your heart, — for your lips had lost their power of prayer, — 'Help me!'

"You thought He did not hear, for no help came. There was no way out. Friends, father, mother, the little sister you loved so dearly, even He to whom you had once knelt — all had forgotten you.

"Oh, to think of that night! No hour since then stands out in the very blackness of darkness as that last hour in the drawing-room! —

"For once they have forgotten you. The door is unlocked! Hush! Down the back stairs — hark, somebody is coming — quick — the area door —

"What a long breath you drew when you stood in the open air — free!

"What creatures are those clutching at you from out the darkness! Brush them away — fight them — don't be dragged back to prison — they are gone!

"You stood upon the pavement — homeless. Ah, *homeless!*

"Then — then it was you who forgot them

— father, mother, Nellie — even Him beyond
whose redemption you thought you had flung
yourself.

"There, dear, don't cry. I'm sorry for
you. I'll help you. Come home with me.
Begin again. Think of your father — he
doesn't care? Your mother! How will you
meet Nellie?

"Don't stand there shivering in that thin
gown. It's a beautiful gown, but it cost you
what you may never have again. You're not
the first, child, I've brought home out of the
cold and wet, and given a good hot cup of tea
and made comfortable in a warm room, till
by and by the despair wasn't quite so deep.
You knew somebody cared.

"Ah, do come, dear. You shall stay with
me till you get work.

"The tobacco factory, was it? Yes, my
child, I know what that means. The air is
suffocating; the dust gives one a racking
cough, and the finger-tips are sore and bleeding. It was the worst of trades, too, for such
as you, so young and pretty! Fine ladies
may understand life's pretty pictures. What
do they know of its realities? With just one
word you could change it all. Why not?
Nobody cared.

"But somebody does care. By and by the
other pictures will fade away and the great

white light will shine upon one face and form —

" You'll come home with me? That's right."

The old woman's fingers grasped the sharp, pointed " sloyd" knife that lay upon the bench; pushing the chair beneath the picture, slowly and carefully she began cutting the canvas from the frame.

" It is such a bitter night for this bare neck — and those thin shoes — how the icy pavement must cut your feet!

" Take my shawl — no, no, it does not matter about me. I've lived through many a night of biting cold, when nobody wanted any scrubbing done. I was too old and stiff for anything else, and I could not beg.

" Let me fasten the shawl for you — There, dear, so — come ! "

. . . .

Rev. Francis Bache was seated at his study table, upon which lay the letter containing the formal call to the great city church. Little as he was accustomed to idleness, for hours he had sat thus, revelling not more in the realization of his dreams of the past and in visions of the future, than in the mere sense of dominant mental power — that intoxication of the intellect compared to which sensual enjoyments are as a child's pleasure in a toy.

There was a knock at the door. "A man, on some urgent errand, wished to see the rector," said the maid. It was the janitor of the Industrial School. From his confused and excited statement, it appeared that after attending to the furnaces for the night, he had made his customary round of the building. On reaching the "sloyd" room, he beheld the portrait by Hunt, with the canvas cut from the frame.

Mr. Bache, as he drew on his overcoat, asked the names of the ladies who had been in charge of the exhibition during the day.

Mrs. De Long, aghast at the rector's tidings, could give no clue to the perpetrator of the outrage. She was certain that she and Mrs. Morris were the last persons in the room, and that the janitor had locked the door of the building after them. "Was she sure of her statement? Might not some one have crept in unobserved in the twilight?" Mrs. De Long repeated, reiterated, and hesitated. Mr. Bache pressed the question.

"The old woman who did the scrubbing about the building had strayed into the room at the last hour" —

She got no further; the next minute Mr. Bache and the janitor were on the pavement, facing the quarter where old Betty lived. There, even in the storm and at the late hour, women, with shawls drawn over their heads, were loitering along the muddy sidewalk, and men and half-grown boys were smoking and talking in loud voices and ribald language on the street corners.

They paused before a miserable tenement-house. The rector lifted the latch of the boltless, lockless door, and strode ahead through an entry in which the tracks of many feet had converted the mud into a slime with which the very walls seemed to reek. A heavy, cold moisture, like that of an underground cave, filled the air, penetrating even through Mr. Bache's luxurious overcoat. Matches were necessary to light the way up three flights of narrow, winding stairs; then, following an entry that plunged into the darkness on the left, the two men reached the room where old Betty lived.

There was no response to the rector's repeated knock, and he pushed the door gently open. The janitor, wondering and impatient, despite his profound reverence, would have crowded near, but Mr. Bache motioned him back.

"Go," he whispered imperiously, and stood alone upon the threshold.

Before him was a fireless room, with the

ceiling just high enough to escape the law's enactments; patches and shreds of discolored paper hung from the dingy walls; a bed, whose outlines the scanty coverlids could not soften; a rusty stove, with a tea-pot and cracked tea-cup upon it; a rickety table, and two battered wooden chairs, comprised the furniture.

Opposite, upon the mantel-shelf, was the object that had riveted the rector's gaze, — the portrait by Hunt. Again, the picture filled the room.

Before it crouched old Betty, talking in disjointed phrases, while her fingers plucked aimlessly at the frozen folds of her gown.

" She called you 'a painted creature,' and left you to the cold and dark. But One who was writing on the ground whispered, 'Never are there gifts so utterly wasted but that, with my help, they may still be used in my service; never was there a life that was wrecked beyond my redemption.'

" It's been — such — a terrible dream. But it's over now. How did it begin? I remember — when they took the portrait from the wall.

" There, Nellie dear, don't cry. You have your own life to live, child, and I must not be a part of it, even in memory. You must not let the shadow of my life fall upon yours.

You have another to live for. Hark! he is
calling you — loosen your arms, dear —

"No, no, it's all a dream —

"There is the portrait, just as it always
was —

"Oh, how the sight of that blank wall
pierced my heart! Why did they take the
picture away? I wish I could get that dream
out of my head.

"Who — brought — the picture back?

"I wish — Francis — would come.

"I wonder — what makes — me — so tired
to-night? — Why — doesn't — Francis —
come!

"Francis! — I knew you would come. I
have waited — so — long — for you, dear.
Let me look at you — so — so.

"It — is good — to rest — my head once
more upon your shoulder!"

"Do you remember that evening we met,
Francis? I wore the pink gown — the one
in the picture — and you said I was —
'adorable.' It was when we stood — by the
door — after the waltz — and you — were
fanning me. I always liked that feather fan,
because your hand had held it.

"I laughed at you, then, so many had
called me 'adorable.' But that night I lay
awake and said the word over and over to
myself. It was a new word — one you had

coined — never spoken to another. Bend
your head — I want to whisper. Tell me
— again, I am adorable !
  " Francis — you who are so true — you
will — tell — me — the truth.
  " Who —brought— the—picture—back? "
  "Why — do — you — turn away —
your face?
  " Was it I — I — who bore it — all — the
long, hard way, back —back to its place —
in my father's mansion? "

    .   .   .   .

  It was long after midnight when Mr. Bache
sat again at his study table. For years after,
his people spoke of that last sermon. The
spare, refined gestures, the eloquent pauses,
the peculiar directness with which he seemed
to address each individual in the great congregation — with all those charms they were familiar. But there was something to-day behind
voice and manner that they felt for the first
time — something which seemed to answer an
unvoiced cry from their inmost natures.
  Great was the surprise when it was known
that Mr. Bache had declined the call he had
received ; greater still when it was heard that
he had left the pulpit forever and would
merge his individuality in that of a brother-
hood whose work lay in the slums of a distant city.

"It was his noble spirit of self-sacrifice," said Mrs. Morris.

"Something lay behind it," thought Mrs. De Long, and dwelt again on those burning words, familiar, yet elusive, with which that last wonderful sermon had closed.

"Even in that saddest failure, which the world mocks by calling success, never are there gifts so utterly wasted but that, with His help, they may still be used in His service; never was there a life that was wrecked beyond His redemption!"

THE FIRST EDITION OF THIS BOOK CONSISTS
OF ONE THOUSAND COPIES PRINTED DURING
OCTOBER 1896 BY THE ROCKWELL AND
CHURCHILL PRESS OF BOSTON

www.ingramcontent.com/pod-product-compliance
Lightning Source LLC
Chambersburg PA
CBHW031106020726
47495CB00007B/2070